THICK AND FAST

By Tommy Dakar

Copyright 2013

Other books by **Tommy Dakar**

<u>Balls</u> – a full length comedy novel

<u>The Trap-Door</u> – literary fiction

<u>A World Apart and other stories</u> – A collection of short stories, most of which have been chosen for publication in literary magazines

<u>Falls the Shadow</u> – Twin stories, separate but inseparable. Literary fiction.

Visit **TOMMY DAKAR**'s website.

www. tommydakar.wix.com/tommydakar

Table of Contents

'Proclaim human equality as loudly as you like. Witless will serve his brother'

Thomas Huxley

'Is there such a thing as wisdom, or is what seems such merely the ultimate refinement of folly?'

Bertrand Russell

This is a true story, which means that not a word of it is to be trusted. All of it has been made up, none of it actually happened, the characters never existed as portrayed. The minute we open our mouths to speak or put pen to paper, the lies begin. We edit and falsify, underline and undermine, put words into people's mouths that were never said, imposing on events a retrospective order to make everything more comprehensible.

Once recounted, everything is invention, pure fiction. Even so, it makes more sense to us than the chaos of fleeting reality.

This is a true story. Don't believe a word of it.

1

He could have been born in the wrong place at the wrong time. He could have been born into the wrong coloured skin, the wrong sex, the wrong social class. No such luck. Ambrose Ork was born thick.

Which meant that ahead of him lay a life of drudgery, humiliation and ridicule without the slightest chance of anyone championing his cause. For nobody pities the dimwitted. Quite the opposite, their inferior IQ is exploited mercilessly, because ignorance is bliss, and it is reasoned that if they are too slow to realise that they are being taken for a ride, then no harm done. They are euphemistically referred to as unqualified labour, and have been brought into this world to clean, haul, dredge, and serve. Brave New World, it would seem, was not a futuristic novel after all.

He was not retarded, had no medically recognised syndrome, was not mentally disabled in any way that needed special treatment and care. Had that been the case he may have received professional attention, some sympathy, compensation even. No such luck. Ambrose Ork was average thick.

Who will fight for the emancipation of the boneheads? Unlike other victimised groups they can never have a clear-sighted leader, they will never be able to organise themselves effectively. Even if they did by some miracle manage to achieve that, they would still not necessarily realise they had been freed. Quite as easily they could be duped, informed that the good fight had been won, liberty restored, their worth recognised, and none the wiser. Discrimination based on race had no future, as it was inevitable that the unjustly stigmatised would eventually rise up against their oppressors and claim their rightful place in society. Women around the world will one day put a stop to glass ceilings and illogical differentiation. Minority groups will bang on doors and demand to be heard until at last, often at long last it is true, their revindications are finally satisfied. But what hope is there for the simple-minded? They are no longer children, to be loved and cared for. They are responsible adults, accountable for their actions, and have to prove their worth before rewards are offered. There is nothing about them physically that provokes pity or understanding, or suggests specific aid. Indeed Ambrose had been a very attractive, athletic man in his youth. They are just big oafs, slow off the mark, easily led, inarticulate and gullible, and therefore, according to the majority of humanity, deserve what they get - the shitty end of the stick.

Slow, dull-witted, half-sharp, there were any number of unflattering adjectives to describe Ambrose's under average intelligence, some of the harsher versions even slipping into insult. Over the years he had become accustomed to hearing those words applied to him, sometimes mumbled, sometimes thrown into his face, and although they still often hurt, as much as sticks and stones despite what they say, he no longer automatically accepted their implicit accusation. It was his humble opinion that on more than one occasion he had been used as a scapegoat, that maybe he wasn't as stupid as some people thought, that some finger-pointing people were not as clever as they'd like us to think. Apart from the obvious case in hand, (today's plan, his long awaited revenge), Mr. Cummings, the world's greatest head waiter, sprang to mind. Perhaps, looking back, more than one of them should take the plank out of their own eye.

He turned the corner and was delighted to see how the dusty red bus strained to a halt under the shade of the huge trees that lined Newby Avenue, trees whose names Ambrose never could remember. His father had pointed them out to him many a time, showing him the difference in the shape of the leaves, the texture of the bark, the variety of seed pods and the like, but he had never been very good at that sort of thing. Elm, beech, birch? He let it go and boarded the bus. He was pleasantly surprised to see that virtually all of the seats on the left side of the vehicle were free, the other passengers preferring to cram themselves into the row on the right for some reason or other. That was fine by him, as he still saw getting a window seat as a kind of prize. It wasn't very far to Chester Drive, just a few miles along the coast, but he would travel in comfort and style, with a view of the sea to boot. Omens, Pet, and all on my side.

As he waited for the driver to finish his spreadsheets and start the ride, he thought back to Mr. Cummings. He had been working in the kitchens of the Golden Nugget, a fast food franchise that gave short term, low paid employment to whoever was desperate enough to take it. Most of the staff were students, washing dishes or taking orders at the counter to pay for their whims and vices, and very few lasted more than a couple of months. Except for Alex, Mr. Cummings to his underlings, who was the full time, reasonably paid overseer. It was his task to see that all those lazy, slovenly, cowardly students were pushed just a little too far, made to do chores and hours above and beyond the call of duty. That way the bosses, three smug, interchangeable brothers whose main concerns in life were profit and leisure, would keep him on, maybe even give him a Christmas bonus.

It was a symbiotic relationship. The brothers could never imagine ever finding such a loyal, hard working, nasty supervisor in a million years. On his c.v. it even stated that he had, for a time, worked in an exclusive French restaurant in Vernon. He was perfect. For his part Alex enjoyed every moment of his new gained power. He had been ridiculed in that fancy restaurant, humiliated, made to look a fool, and eventually squeezed out. That would now be the fate of his arrogant, on-the-way-to success student work force. Once bitten, twice a biter. Thank you Mr. Cummings, the brothers would say once the monthly accounts had been successfully completed. It is my pleasure, he would reply, sincerely.

Ambrose had taken the job on his sister's insistence. Their parents were both dead and although they could manage on her wage for the time being, a little extra income would be much appreciated. Anyway, it was time for Ambrose to earn his keep.

He soon became the arse to be kicked. The students acted towards him in much the same way as Mr. Cummings, bawling him out, never giving him a minute's peace, leaving the worst jobs for him, the dibbo without exams. He was also expected to be first in and last out, and if anything went wrong he was almost sure to take the blame, guilty or not. Ambrose lived in fear of losing his first job, and did everything he was told to do, and more if he had the time and energy. He saw how the students came and went, some fired, others after a shouting match with Mr. Cummings, others through boredom or sheer fatigue. It was only a matter of time, he thought, before this Mr. Cummings called him to his office and threw his cards at him. Then what would he say to Petunia? He need not have worried. Alex Cummings was overjoyed with his new staff member, it was what he had always coveted. A semi slave who lived in fear of him, who never answered back, who never refused to do even the most menial, degrading task. A dog to whip. It was too good to be true, and although in public he tortured Ambrose with snappy sarcasm and sneers, in private, and to his bosses, he sang the man's praises. Alex Cummings and Ambrose Ork were set to last for a lifetime.

The bus swung out onto Ocean Way and he soon understood the seating plan. The midday sun burnt into the window of his side of the bus like through a magnifying glass, quickly heating the metal and plastic bus seats until they were almost impossible to touch. Ambrose began to sweat, his T-shirt sticking to his back under his green, gardener's dungarees. He considered changing seats, but was somehow reluctant to recognise his mistake. He had made his decision, now he would have to stick to it, or the others would laugh. 'Can't stand the heat, eh?' 'You've been sitting in the hot seat!' and other smartarse comments. He preferred to let them think that he loved sitting in the sun and watching the sea.

Then, quite inexplicably, one hot summer's day, Mr. Cummings made a terrible mistake. The chickens used to create the franchise's breadcrumbed one hundred percent poultry delights arrived deep frozen, presented on sterilised white plastic trays, and covered hygienically in cling film. They were as hard as rock. 'Whole Chicken' the packages read, though in reality they had already been beheaded, plucked, their feet and wings removed, their innards sold on for other, unnameable uses. What remained had been neatly cut and arranged to make nugget and drumstick preparing a less labour intensive task. It had been Alex Cumming's intention to slightly defrost the chickens, take a little hardness out of them thereby accelerating the thawing process, then, when they had been softened up, put them back into cold store. It was only a very subtle bending of health and safety regulations, and of little or no importance if done correctly. Certainly no more than an hour two at the most. Because, as he had screamed so often to his moronic subordinates, the cold chain must never, never, be broken. It was the golden rule of catering. But that day he had entirely forgotten about the chickens, had dismissed everybody, Ambrose included, and sent them all home until Tuesday. That had been on Sunday evening; the Golden Nugget was always closed on Mondays.

When Ambrose had opened up the following Tuesday he had been met by a particularly cloying stench. Huge flies buzzed orgasmicly round the soft, pink-brown, dripping flesh of the rotting carcasses, which had burst their transparent wrappings as if trying to escape. There must have been over fifty dead birds putrefying on that stainless steel ledge, more than a day's worth of golden nuggets fit for no more than the bin. Lara had arrived next, and had helped Ambrose tidy up the mess. They both knew who had slipped up, but who would have the guts to say so? Ambrose knew who would eventually get the blame, and for a few minutes was able to accept that reality, his schooling had helped prepare him for such events. But when the furious, hypocritical Mr. Cummings had the gall to fly into a terrible rage and hurl abuse at him, it was more than he could take. 'It wasn't me?', he said, trembling a little at his audacity, but stubborn too, 'it was your fault. You forgot to put them back into cold store, not me'. It was the first time Ambrose had retorted to his supervisor, and it would be his last. Whilst Mr. Cummings, the ex head waiter of a reputable French restaurant launched into a tirade against the incompetence of young Mr. Ork, Ambrose took off his apron, tossed it onto the work surface, and walked out. 'Where do think you are going? Eh! Come back here this instance, I didn't give you permission to go. Thickhead!'

Looking back he should have punched the fool in the face.

Ocean Way slipped out of the city centre and made its way along the shoreline towards the plush suburbs of the West. Since his last visit he noticed that the coast road had been widened, flowers had been planted, and new lights had been placed overhead like enormous reading lamps. Langley, his destination, was a quiet, discreet, exclusive enclave which kept its distance from the hubbub of the city as if it were above such mundane and frenetic activity. Here it was assumed that people knew their sycamores from their ash. Buses and other means of public transport were only tolerated on the perimeter access routes, whilst inside, along spotless, leafy lanes, a civilised calm reigned supreme.

It had been his father's idea - Ambrose, food of the Gods. The story went that he had seen it in a newspaper, Ambrose somebody-or-other, he couldn't remember now, a wealthy businessman of sorts, a self-made hero of the times. A simple, honest type who had risen from rags to riches, from misery to economic happiness by investing, or buying and selling, or something like that. It was all about tycoons and fortunes and fabulous inheritances, and Ambrose had never been able to fully understand the plot, but his father had obviously hoped that his son would be inspired by such an optimistic yarn. He'd had a belief that a name could make or break you. He had known so many nondescript types called Nigel or Graham, so many athletic empty heads named Scott or Greg, a host of untrustworthy Denises and Leslies. He had preferred bold, forceful Mikes, know-where-you stand Steves, everyday Johnnies and Jims. But for his son he had wanted something special, something that would make him stand out in a crowd, something that would inspire people to doff their hats and make room for him as he passed. His mother had disliked the idea from the start and had put up token resistance, but having had her way with the naming of his elder sister, she didn't have a leg to stand on. Had his father known that his offspring, his sole male heir, would not turn out to be the sharpest pencil on the desk he might have had pity on him and called him something forgettable like Joe. Alas, Ambrose Ork it was.

Ambrose felt nervous. He knew perfectly well which stop was his, yet he could not avoid imagining that he would make a terrible mistake; get off too soon and have to hike miles along the hot, dangerous hard shoulder of the motorway, or miss his stop altogether and end up in... who knows where? What if the setting down point had been changed? What if the driver forgot to stop? What if he took too long getting to the door, and the bus pulled away while he was half in, half out? He would break a leg and have to go to hospital, and then the whole scheme would just screw up. It was incredibly hot stuck up against that window, and his heavy dungarees clung to him like a damp towel. Crawford Bridge, Blume, Upper Cowdale Metal, Lexington Mall. He knew them by heart, but still he had to be careful, remain alert, keep his mind on the task in hand. Today of all days he could not afford a blunder.

Well before time Ambrose stood up and made his way to the

back door. He wanted the driver to be able to see him in his rear view mirror, just in case the buzzer hadn't sounded, or he hadn't seen the red Next Stop sign lighted up in his cabin. What if nobody else wanted to get off, what if there was no-one waiting to get on? Would the driver just carry on down the highway, leaving Ambrose in a state of panic, his plan ruined? Better safe than sorry. Anyway, he enjoyed the swaying movements of the bus, its boat like swelling and dipping, its sudden surges and swerves. It was exhilarating and challenging, like dancing to a strange new tune whose rhythm it was hard to catch.

The world over a fool and his money are easily parted. Ambrose and his sister Petunia could unfortunately corroborate that. Maybe he wouldn't even be there today if it wasn't for the likes the Wiggins. The mentally dense are too often considered easy meat, to be preyed upon by unscrupulous, untrustworthy people who cynically gain the confidence of their unwitting victims then quickly dash off with their spoils. The culprits claim that it is purely survival of the fittest, the fastest in this case, and that if nature has arranged things thus, who are they to criticise? So thousands of unwitting souls are skinned alive every year by those lucky enough to have been born with a decent dollop of grey matter in their skulls. If it happens once, there is general sympathy, but after a second or third incident cold judgement is passed – they must be stupid. All compassion ends there. Fools are not suffered gladly.

He jumped off the bus just before it pulled to a halt. He knew it was not the right thing to do, that he should wait until the vehicle had come to a complete standstill, that it was dangerous and foolhardy. But he couldn't help it, it was something he had always enjoyed doing despite continual parental admonishments. 'You'll break your legs one of these days', 'You'll fall flat on your face and knock out your teeth, then what?' Nothing had ever happened.

He checked his watch. He would be there much sooner than they had originally planned, as he had decided to take the earlier bus to avoid unseen snags like accidents, traffic jams, roadblocks and the like. But arriving before time could only work to his advantage. It was what Spotty would call a contingency. He remembered his old cell mate Spotty drilling him, quizzing him, the light glinting off his spectacles, his shiny head and keen eyes trained on his apprentice, like a well-fed Ghandi with a goatee. What if the bus didn't stop, eh? What if it burst a tyre, or over-heated, or was hijacked by desperados? What if a van had crashed and spilt toxic waste over the highway? What then, Bro? Well it wouldn't have necessarily spelt disaster, because Ambrose had taken it into account, had taken the contingency. Now he could take his time.

Across the dual carriageway Langley, like a tycoon on a sun bed, languished in its sea of green, rising up slightly so as to enjoy a privileged view of the immense azure ocean, today as calm as a kidney shaped pool. Somewhere behind that curtain of bright green leaves, a little to the right of the towers of the Golf Club, lay Haute House. Ambrose took a deep breath. He had to control himself, to control his memories. Stick to the plan, think of nothing else. He would try.

He crossed the busy road at the lights and headed up Chester Drive, past imposing metal driveway doors, surveillance cameras and madly barking guard dogs, towards the wrought iron main gates of the mansion. It was deserted now, as the family, or what was left of it, would be at their summer house on Kenton Beach. The gardeners would be in three times a week, but today was Thursday, so he would have the place to himself. He followed a narrow path which ran alongside the crumbling perimeter wall on its way to the grounds at the back of the house, and eventually on to Walcott Way. When he reached the agreed point he stooped to retie his boot laces, quickly made sure he was unseen, then neatly leapt up on to the wall. He was up and over in a second under the protection of a fully clothed willow tree.

It was difficult to say when his parents had first noticed that something was amiss with young Ambrose. He had started off fine, learning to walk before his first birthday, cutting teeth with apparent ease. He had been healthy and strong, and the doctors had praised them for their good fortune. His appetite was legendary. While Petunia picked at her food with disdain, as if it were out of date medicine, Ambrose ate whatever was put before him without complaint. Mr. George Ork was sure that at this rate his son would gobble up the whole world by the time he was ten. A giant of finance had been born! That would have fulfilled George Ork's wildest dreams, for Ambrose's father longed more than anything to be rich, preferably indecently rich, because like most of his contemporaries he confused security and comfort with happiness. But by the time he was two, two and a half, the child had still not learnt to speak above a dozen words. They were told not to worry, but they did. They thought of taking him to specialists, but friends, family, everybody they knew agreed there was nothing wrong with the boy – he would learn soon enough.

And so he did, slowly.

He sat under the protection of the willow and waited. It was unlikely that he had been spotted, but if he had, or if new cameras had been installed, then he would know soon enough. The dogs, if they still had any, would have been taken to Kenton Beach too, or put into one of those dog hotels, but again, better safe than sorry. If somehow they had been left behind to guard the place then they would pick up his scent and come investigating before ten minutes was up. He checked his watch again and felt a glow of adventure, as if he were a commando on a daring raid. Synchronise watches. He had even done that with Spotty, to practice, and it had filled him with pride. He would give it ten, no twelve, minutes. Time for a cigarette? he had asked. Only if you are extremely careful and don't blow smoke everywhere or leave the butt lying around. Think of DNA samples. Think of snipers. Ambrose hadn't understood that final remark, but was too embarrassed to say so.

School had unmasked him. Until then he had only been compared to his elder sister Petunia, not destined for the intellectual life herself, but far more able, awake and alert than her little brother. Naturally, argued their parents; she was a year and half older. However it soon became apparent that Ambrose belonged in the slow lane. Most of his classmates seemed to have crystal clear minds made up of a fascinating transparent liquid. Ambrose waded through thick sludge. Some of his best friends had prisms in their eyes through which they saw an incredible, cinemascopic reality. Ambrose couldn't see past the end of his nose, as his mother often reminded him. The alphabet was like a never ending slope, eventually leading you upwards to a summit from where you could discern a swollen sea of unspellable words, thousands upon thousands of them all waiting to be memorised. Once a number of words had been correctly assimilated, they suddenly required new, confusing definitions, had to be categorised into adjectives and adverbs, thereby throwing everything once more into disarray. So reading made him feel dizzy, as if he were about to fall into that ocean of sentences and paragraphs, where he would thrash around uselessly until he drowned.

He fared no better at maths. Sums teased you at first with their innocent simplicity, filled you with false confidence, only to get harder and harder until they became deliberately unfriendly, malicious even. The torture was incessant. Addition and subtraction gave way to multiplication and division, to fractions and decimals, and from there relentlessly onwards into the unknown. Only the most intrepid dared to follow, only the naturally gifted could manage to keep up. Petunia flagged a little, but did not lose sight of the main group that cut through the undergrowth always a few hundred yards ahead of her. But Ambrose soon got lost, and decided he was better off back in base camp where everything was safe and familiar.

His ten minutes were up; so far so good. He strolled across the lawn as if he had every right to be there, as Spotty had told him that was the best way to go unnoticed, and made his way up to the porch. He could see his sister Petunia, stuffed into her best Sunday dress, still sweating and puffing from the slight climb up the hill to the magnificent Victorian, or Edwardian, or some other style house. Today our luck is going to change, she had said. It had certainly seemed that way at the time.

Señora Luz had opened the door. She was a small, dark woman with an air of seriousness verging on pain. Dressed in a maid's uniform, her black hair slicked back into a tight pony tail, she had tried not to let them see that she was sizing them up and evaluating their worth, as if she herself were the employer. Petunia had started to introduce herself, but she'd got no further than 'good day' when Señora Luz had cut her short with a monotone 'follow me'.

That had been their first lesson. Instead of leading them through the main doors, the middle aged maid, all in black except for her beautifully made white apron, had led them round the side of the mansion to the service area. It was something they had not expected, and it had struck them both as extremely rude. Ambrose had made little signs to his sister as if to ask what was going on, but Petunia had begged him with her eyes to behave himself and say nothing. So they had scurried behind the maid as best they could, trying their best to look calm and dignified. Later, back in the bedsit, she would try to explain it all to herself by pretending to be explaining it to Ambrose, a handy habit she had picked up during her childhood.

'Some people think they're superior, Bro. They think that just 'cause they've got money they are better than you. Others think that they're a better class of person, the high and mighty, just because they was born in the right place at the right time. They're the sort of person that won't show you in through the main hall, but take you round the back, as if you was a servant, because they think you're not worthy or something.'

She flashed him a smile, her eyes sparkling.

'If we suddenly win the lottery they'll want to know us alright, they'd throw open the doors and throw us a banquet.'

Then, frowning.

'That's the way they are, Bro.'

Señora Luz had hurried past the conservatory and garages in the noonday heat to a side door, Petunia and Ambrose trotting behind her as composedly as possible in their awkward clothes, along a narrow corridor, and had eventually shown them into a small office. Wait here.

It had been so hot in there! But Petunia had insisted that he keep his jacket on – appearances were so important to this type of person. That morning she had dressed him as if he were her only son about to begin his first day at a new college. She had ironed and brushed and fussed over his clothes until she was resignedly as happy as could be expected at the outcome, given the circumstances and the raw materials at hand. Then she had turned her attention to his hair, his thick, dark brown hair, with its tufts and crinks that, if not exactly rebellious, was at least disobedient. Finally she had declared him fit for human consumption. Then he'd had to wait until she had completed the same ritual with herself. The result had been slightly comical.

'You look like you're going to a wedding, Pet.'

'And you look like you're about to be brought before the judge.'

The 'office' was really no more than a small storage room which had been decorated with a desk, a leather swivel chair, and a computer. A poorly painted window gave out onto a brick wall, and Pet was a little surprised to see that the walls were totally bare – not even a calendar. She was unsure if that was a good sign or not. First they had been interviewed by Mr. Stein, a clean, well-groomed, short man in his fifties, like the office itself without a trace of humour or humanity, with sharp eyes that scrutinised them from behind metal framed glasses. Mr. Stein didn't clip the hairs that grew out of his ears, Petunia couldn't help noticing, and that seemed incongruent. Perhaps, she had thought at the time, it was also a sign, an omen. They would not get the jobs. But no, there were other, more potent signals, of that she was sure, so she should not worry. He read through their references as if he had already caught them out and was about to call the police. Like a detective he went over the main points again and again, firing questions at Petunia, then turning to watch Ambrose's face while she answered. They had laughed about it all later, but at the time he had come across as a stern prosecuting lawyer and had scared the wits out of both of them. Then Stein had disappeared without a word, and left them to sweat it out.

The porch was exactly as he had remembered it; elegant, imposing, but just a little bit too old world, too aged, too rancid. It smacked of butlers and hunting parties, of inherited money and unearned social status. The woodwork was in a poor state of repair, much worse than when he had been in charge of its conservation, and the ironwork needed priming or it would just rust away. He climbed up the marble steps and turned to take in the view. He imagined his father putting his arm round his shoulders and saying, in the mocking tone he had so often adopted when talking to his son, 'one day Ambrose all this will be yours.' The clipped and harnessed gardens, the curtsying and bowing trees, the wide sweep of the ocean. He realised his mouth was open, and quickly closed it. Best get round the back before he called attention to himself.

Finally Stein had returned and led them through some double doors to the main hall of the house, and from there into an exquisite, lemon yellow room they later learned was called the morning room. Mrs. Haute in person had received them. They had been overawed, as they had in no way expected to actually meet the lady of the house, let alone have to talk to her. They stood to attention while Mr. Stein explained in a few brief sentences who they were and what their lives up to that moment amounted to. It had been a nerve racking and embarrassing experience, especially when she had motioned for them to sit down on a doll's house settee that looked as though it would break under Petunia's ample folds, and Ambrose's sturdy frame. But she had been gracious and witty, doing her best to come across as modern, down to earth and not at all out of touch with the real world and its problems. Hence the loose fitting blouse and designer jeans, the bobbed hair and subtle make-up. She had been friendly in a distant, posh way, as she had been back then, and after a very awkward moment when orange refreshment had been offered, she let them know that they had been conditionally accepted. Stein would later inform them of the details in his office. Salary, accommodation, holidays – a job, two jobs, starting next Monday.

The burglar alarm would be on, but he knew how to fix that, with or without official diplomas. After all, he had installed it. He walked past the conservatory and round the back to the garages.

That first day had been so intense, so fast, that they had not really taken it all in. They had been in a daze, as if a fairy godmother had turned their shabby clothes into gowns of golden thread. If they had met Señora Luz at the market they would have walked straight past her, swearing they had never seen her before in their lives. Stein had stuck in their minds only as a negative sensation, and Mrs. Haute had appeared before them as if through the haze of a movie camera, slightly unreal and ephemeral, as if about to suddenly wave her wand and vanish.

'That day changed our lives, Bro'

Petunia was fond of repeating, though whether she meant for better or for worse Ambrose could not say. Better for her, maybe.

Under the privet hedge that ran down the far side of the garages was the control box, the original one, the one he had been ordered to put in by Harvey, with all the fuses neatly laid out in rows. From here he could do what he liked with the electricity in the mansion. Like turn off the burglar alarm, unqualified as he was. Time and weather had all but erased the writing on the labels, but he knew which fuses to remove. He looked over the gardens just in case, though he was sure he was alone and unobserved, because in Langley it was not done to spy on one's neighbours, this was not the barbecue belt. He knew that if he tampered with the burglar alarm fuse, the whole house would jump up and start screaming and shaking with deafening bells, and the security firm, maybe even the local police, would see a little red light flashing on their control panel. But if he blacked out the general fuse first, the one without a label that he had added under his own initiative, just as his father had so painstakingly and patiently shown him, then replaced the alarm fuse with a dud, then switched it all back on....... That should work. Not bad for an amateur. Unless he had overlooked something, Haute House was his for the taking.

He wanted to jump up and down and do a little jig. The plan was being followed to the letter. To the fucking letter, Spotty! Who's the thicky now, eh? Of course, there was still a chance that when he tried to break in the alarm would go off anyway, that he had made some kind of mistake, or that they'd had some new-fangled system installed in his absence, but for now...

It would have been perfect if his parents could have seen him then, triumphant, cunning, a man with a plan orderly carrying it out point by point. He thought back to his Mother, she would have been so proud of him.

Peggy Wilson had become Mrs. Ork at the age of twenty, leading her lover, four years her elder, to believe that he had been the first man who had ever possessed her, for although she usually condemned deceit, in this case she felt herself fully justified. She had made the foolish mistake once of admitting her previous experiences, and Lars, a normally cool, even aloof Adonis, had been transformed in a moment. She had gone from making love to fucking, then to being fucked. She had caught sight of him reflected in the car window, and he had seemed to be trying to break her in two, ramming her with sadistic disgust as if it were a substitute for beating her to the ground with his fists. And enjoying every minute of it. So she had lied to George, trustworthy and trusting George, because she knew that if she chose the right occasion, the right amount of drink and sleeplessness, he would never be able to doubt her word. She also suspected that if he believed he had deflowered her, had been the first man to enter her, it would make him love her even more, respect her for longer, would help to keep him faithful. Her intuition had not been wrong, and apart from wandering eyes and torrid fantasies, George Ork had remained loyal.

To her at least. But George Ork had not shared his wife's unconditional love of their children. He had been bitterly disappointed both by Petunia's looks and Ambrose's intelligence. His daughter was not ugly, not in the classic, repugnant sense some poor creatures have to suffer, but she was definitely not very attractive, either. Her teeth were far too large for her mouth, and when she smiled the cheery effect was ruined by the tombstone aspect of her incisors. Later in life she would become a passionate smoker, and those terrible teeth would turn yellow, her gums would retreat in horror, and even more expanse of unhealthy enamel would be exposed. Her hair grew limp and lacklustre, her eyes were small and round. She had grown fat right from the start, and nothing on earth seemed to be able to reverse that trend. Ungraceful, common, not too bright, easily led... Her father used to shake his head at the thought of her. Which was unfair, because although there was indeed an element of truth in all of his observations and criticisms, he ignorantly glossed over any number of endearing traits that made Petunia much more than a lost opportunity or a failed project.

Ambrose he had appeared to accept as a cross to bear, a punishment for some past sin he had not remembered committing. As the truth had slowly settled, as the exam results had shuffled in, as the learning curve had taken so long to get off the ground, so his father had stoically lowered his head and accepted that the dream of fabulous wealth would have to wait. Inadvertently he had begun to speak to Ambrose in clearly separated monosyllables, patiently at first, later developing that gently mocking tone that he had used until his death.

Only now Ambrose had the fuse box under control, which meant he had the house under control, which meant he had the whole plan under control. He felt sure his father would have approved.

That first Monday had brought them back to earth. They may have been given a job, they may have been offered lodgings, food, some cash at the end of the month, but they would earn every last cent.

Cleanliness is next to godliness, but cleaning is for the low born or the braindead, as Petunia had known all her life. She had scrubbed and dusted and mopped her way through hundreds of underpaid jobs over the years, just like her mother before her. That was what awaited unskilled labourers, men and women with no qualifications or aptitudes, no exceptional skills, no contacts. Still, no point complaining. She counted her blessings and got on with the tasks in hand under Señora Luz's suspicious vigilance. Ambrose was to be in charge of every menial chore that Stein considered he was capable of completing without making matters worse, especially if it involved getting dirty or lugging things about from place to place. But the Orks were used to hard labour, it was their birthmark. They toiled silently and efficiently from dawn to dusk, and once their trial period was up, they were welcomed into the household as full time staff.

Haute House. Most people had trouble pronouncing it at first, and were unsure whether it was said by dropping the 'h' to rhyme with Oat, as in haute cuisine, which was the officially correct form, or if it was the more common but more logical

Hout. That was not how it was pronounced in those parts, as the locals were happy and proud to point out. Neither was it, as one of Mrs. Haute's closest rivals had so wittily put it, Haugh-ty, as in whore with a tea. The surname Haute had been simplified through the years and the local accent to 'Out', so the place was consequently referred to as Out House, probably with the idea in mind of bringing the self important family down a peg or two.

The mansion was one of a number of others that had been built over a century ago, all on the same grassy slopes, all overlooking the bay on the right side of town, because birds of a feather flock together and the rich need wealthy neighbours like a model needs a full length mirror. It boasted a golf club whose membership fees were set to make it unassailable by mere mortals, and a chapel, complete with spire and graveyard, to date sparsely populated. As Ambrose made his way towards the service entrance, he couldn't help but notice how the place seemed so much older now, in great need of repair. Weeds grew out of the roof tiles and had blocked the guttering, so the rain water was forced to spill out and run down the walls leaving dark, streaky stains as if the place had been crying. Some of the window panes were cracked, and the shutters badly needed painting. The late Mrs. Haute would never have let the place run to rot like this.

Still, the gardens were looking magnificent. They had been designed by some famous landscape gardener, quite an expensive authority at the time though Ambrose couldn't remember his name now, or when it had been initiated, or if this was the original design, or if there had been a remodelling over the years. It had all been explained and discussed in the long summer nights at Haute House, but he had trouble retaining information, especially if it were in the slightest way technical, or historical, or anything that smacked of school subjects. Brendan had been responsible for all that until his retirement. Now it would be Brendan's son. Or grandson, even. They could charge people to come and see this, he thought, there was not a tree or a plant that was not at its best, perfectly pruned and trimmed. The man had been a genius in his own way, he meant Brendan, and it looked like it ran in the family.

The white painted door with its round brass door knob was locked, so he smashed his elbow through one of the six frosted glass panes of the door. Nothing. This was to be his second pause. If a new alarm had been put in, it may just be that it did not ring there and then, not in the house itself. It had sounded odd to Ambrose, but Spotty had assured him such things existed, and he should know. He had told Ambrose of infra-red rays and heat detectors, amazing technology that could pick up a mouse breathing under the floorboards and work out its weight and average speed, all carried out in perfect silence. The idea was to let the burglar think he was safe, giving time for the cops, or some private security firm, to get over there and catch the poor bastard red-handed. So he now had to go back to the garages and wait, preferably down by the hedge, and see if anybody turned up. Give it ten minutes, have a smoke if you like, care-full-y, he had said. If nothing has happened by then, you're in.

When George Ork had been asked 'what do you do?', he had always wanted to answer, 'oh, I go for a run on Sundays, and I like to have a little bet on the horses now and then, not too much, just enough to feel a win would be great, but that losing wouldn't be the end of the world. And you?' Instead he said he was an electrician. That information was supposed to help describe him, to give an idea of his worth, of his position in society. It was something he had never got used to. He could never understand why his occupation should be of so much interest, or use, to everyone. In his time he had been a student, an amateur boxer, an insurance salesman, a dishwasher, an apprentice car mechanic-cum-painter, and finally an electrician. His wife Peggy had been a secretary, a housewife, a part-time cleaner. They had ridden up and down the social scale depending on circumstances, receiving either acceptance and congratulations (I'm in insurance and my wife works for a legal firm), or condolences and resignation (I spray-paint bodywork and my wife is a cleaner). So when he had realised that Ambrose would not be taking his place in the hall of fame and fortune, he had decided to teach him a trade so that he would have something to add as an appendage to his surname. From that moment on Ambrose was to accompany him whenever possible, and even if it took forever, the boy was to learn the basics of electricity.

As suspected the burglar alarm had effectively been neutralised, so he went back to the door, put his hand, carefully, don't leave any DNA, through the smashed glass, and tried to open it from the inside. He had vaguely hoped that whoever was now in charge of such things would have left the key in the lock, just as he used to do when had worked there, but it was not to be; he would have to force his way in after all. He went back to the garage area and snooped around until he found something he hoped would do the trick. With the aid of a large stone and a thick, short piece of metal, by the look of it part of some kind of gardening tool, he managed, not without breaking into a sweat, to gouge open a gash in the woodwork on the inside of the door frame, and then with a huge push he was in.

At that moment his father would have smiled, sighed, and punched him on the shoulder. 'You see, it's not so difficult after all.' By which he had meant that everything in life was a matter of memorising sequences. If you started at the beginning, then methodically, with full concentration, followed the steps one by one, you could not help but end up with a completed task, a job well done. It was like counting. Start at one, don't skip any numbers, keep going steadily, and you'll get to a hundred in no time. Even Ambrose could do it. Maybe not the first time, maybe not even after god knows how many attempts, maybe not until his father had sworn at him, told him to pay attention, called him a useless, good for nothing idiot, thrown the wire cutters at him, pulled out his hair in exasperation and cursed the day he had been born. But eventually, through patience and the sheer bloody-mindedness of his tutor, Ambrose had been taught the elementary concepts. Now he had broken into a supposedly burglar-proof mansion, was crushing broken glass under his work boots, and the alarm had not gone off. He imagined the experts scratching their heads and saying, with a British, scientific accent, 'remarkable, quite inexplicable'.

The service area, previously known as the servants' quarters, was where he and Petunia had spent most of their time whilst employed by the Haute family. It was at the back of the house, the part that gave on to the garages and the boiler house, small rooms with little or no view of the grounds, functional and painted entirely in white. But they were cosy in winter, and airy in summer, and had become home after so many years. Either way he preferred them to the cold, stuffy, museum like rooms of the rest of the house, full of uncomfortable furniture and dark oil paintings, glass cabinets full of expensive, tasteless junk, ancient wooden trunks with ingenious metal mechanisms, and shelf after shelf of unread dusty tomes. Everything, no matter how ugly, was worth a fortune in that part of the house, and Señora Luz had been responsible for it all. No item, no matter how apparently insignificant, had escaped her nervous eye, and she had kept her personal inventory up to date and under lock and key. Her life, or at least her livelihood, had depended on it.

Ambrose scrutinised the kitchen as if he were a potential buyer, running his finger along the marble work surfaces, opening drawers, checking the cupboards. For a second he pretended to be Sydney, the young master of the house, giving his approval to the staff. Well done Pet, a grand job. Keep it up, Bro.

It was the largest room of the service area, with three perfectly defined parts. There was the original kitchen, with high windows that gave out onto the grounds at the back of the mansion, complete with a wood burning stove and hob, a monumental piece of craftsmanship still used to this day.

Ambrose supposed the cooker must have been put in place before they built the kitchen itself, because it would never have fitted through the doors. The double sink, carved out of a single slab of white marble, or so the legend went, was adorned with high bronze taps that reminded Ambrose of coffee pot spouts. There was a central work table, with copper pots and ladles hanging according to size at a height just enough to clear your head whilst still being in reach of short legged cooks and maids, like Pet. But time moves on relentlessly, and space had to be found for more modern fittings such as dishwashers, microwaves, split level ovens and ice machines, so an extension had been added to house what had gradually become the centre of activity. To the left of the antique zone, forming an L, was the staff dining room, where all the different characters and personalities of those who toiled at Haute House would meet in search of an educated, tolerable balance. And watch TV.

Ambrose had not studied genetics, nor would he have understood it if he had, so he could not know that the DNA of most mammals was virtually identical, and that if an embryo is to produce a chicken wing or a forearm is matter of reading the fine print. He would never have believed it if he had been told that, given the right adjustments, Ambrose himself could have been dismembered and presented on a plastic tray, later to be converted into a golden nugget. We are little more than intelligent chickens. But we are chickens nonetheless, and a pecking order had to be established and kept, or feathers would be ruffled. Joe Stein was head of staff, both officially and unofficially, and try as he might to create a relaxed, feel-at-home atmosphere, he could not dare to forget, or allow others to forget, his professional status. It had taken him a lifetime to achieve, and it had to be maintained at all costs. So he would joke and chat, and lean back in his chair, generously giving his fellow workers enough rope. But at the smallest hint of irreverence, his darting eyes would almost audibly register the misdemeanour, and the room would fall into a momentary silence. Like a priest, he would wait for penitence, in any form, a nervous cough, a lowering of the eyes, an 'as you well know, Mr. Stein', he did not stand on ceremony, and once that had been received and recognised, he would continue as before. Señora Luz took second place, and expected respect from the other members of the household staff much like a grandmother does of her grandchildren. It was in the nature of things, like a love of babies or a fear of rats. She could not have conceived a situation wherein her position was not taken with the respect it deserved, it would have upset her notion of the world and its presumed order. The others seemed to perceive this intuitively, and acted accordingly.

Pet and Bro were the others. As newcomers, as latecomers, as the underlings, theirs was to keep a low profile and follow the leader. Over the years they too would gain a certain amount of respect, affection even, but they were never to forget their place or step out of line, at least not too far out of line, or Stein would throw them a steely glance, and Luz would straighten her back or tighten her lips. Then it would be time for confession. Pet was an old hand at this sort of social bartering, and managed the situation with ease and a certain jollity, but her brother often needed prompting, as he sometimes appeared to be in a world of his own, totally unaware of the nuances of such mature interaction. She would nudge him in the ribs, or jerk her head at him. He would stare back blankly. So she would speak for him. 'What Ambrose meant was .....', to which he would nod his agreement and bow his head in repentance.

That left Brendan the gardener, and his son Brendan, the gardener. But they lived off premises, only working three days a week most of the year, and were seen as outsiders, mavericks, a law unto themselves. They were allowed to air revolutionary views, swear, contradict both Stein and Luz, and get away with it. Because, not being lodged at Haute House, they didn't have to follow the same code of conduct as the inmates. They were free to come and go as they pleased, and therefore to think freely too, as long as they did a decent job and behaved civilly, which they did. Ambrose had admired them so much.

He crossed the kitchen, avoiding the temptation to see if there was anything to eat or drink, as Spotty had instructed him, and took the narrow stairs up to his old room.

He was surprised to find it totally empty. Why would that be? He tried to imagine a chain of events that might have led to his room being vacated, who the last tenant had been, where the furniture was being stored, but he had never been very imaginative, not in a logical sequence one thing leading to another way, so he dropped it. It was empty, and that was that. Without the wardrobe, the bed, the writing desk, it looked absurdly tiny, no bigger than his prison cell, or at least the one at Queens II. His footprints rang out hollowly as he passed over to the window. There was not much to see – the wall and roof of the boiler house, the kitchen windows if you strained your head a little, a slice of lawn. He tried to remember when he had last contemplated that view, but was unable to choose from a number of tense occasions. Either way it had been a nightmare.

Quarter past four. Plenty of time.

One of Petunia's lovers had overheard a conversation one day and given her the tip off. According to him, Bob or something, a pear-shaped man with a baby face and a tattoo on his wrist that resembled a bracelet but was in fact something special, and had to do with the Chinese, an amulet of sorts, Pet would remember. According to him, (Bill, yes it had been Bill Corsair, the taxi driver), the old couple who had been at Haute House for years were finally retiring, and Mrs. Haute would soon be looking for a replacement. Apparently she was not keen on a modern married couple, as they posed the threat of children, infidelity and divorce. A brother and sister would be so much easier to handle. Perhaps for a few favours Bill could have a word with Stein? Petunia loved giving favours, so the interview had been settled there and then, in the tool shed.

Pet had known the jobs were theirs from the start. Apart from the gut feeling, something she had learnt to revere, she'd spread the playing cards on the table and there had been no doubt. If he remembered rightly it had been something about houses and knights and a run of numbers. Anyway, as she had pointed out triumphantly, they had an appointment for the 7th, which was the seventh of the seventh. Ambrose didn't understand about numbers or tides or women, so he had just left it all in his sister's fleshy hands.

It couldn't have come at a better time. It had been over a year since they had been evicted from the family home. The small town house that their parents had taken a lifetime to pay off and had been their only inheritance had been stolen from them by the bank. Just because Pet and Ambrose had used the property as a guarantee. Not even for themselves, but for the Wiggins, so they could start up the bakery. It had all started innocently enough. Jack and Sally Wiggins had come up with a brilliant plan that would definitely make everyone money. The idea was to open a bakery, not any old bakery, but one specialising in organic breads and cakes. They would start with one, but soon the business would blossom into a franchise. Pet and Ambrose were to be offered a stake in one if they would just sign a piece of paper. It was that simple. No money needed, no outlay, just a signature, and their futures would be resolved. Ambrose had urged his sister to take that fatal step, and under pressure from both her brother and the Wiggins, especially Jack, who was a bit of a charmer, she had accepted. What harm could a signature do? If only she had listened to her guts back then. But she had had a soft spot for Jack Wiggins, literally, and that had muddied her instincts. She would try not to let it happen again.

The Wiggins never opened a bakery. Rumour had it they went to Italy on the proceeds; nobody had heard of them since. The bailiffs had come, but The Orks had refused to budge – it was not *their* debt, so it was not fair to evict them, especially as they had nowhere to go. For months they avoided all post, never answered phone calls, kept the doors well-locked, and tried to hold on like a castle under siege. The police were eventually called in to do the dirty work, and the Orks found themselves on the pavement with no more than a couple of suitcases and a wad of official papers.

Bad times. He had heard that most people forget the bad times and only recall the good times. If so, then he must be an exception, either that or the good times were too few and far between.

So the job at Haute House had been a godsend. At the time Ambrose had been unloading ships at the dock, not every day, but enough to keep them both in rent and food. He had worked hard, terribly hard. Being a bit slow off the mark meant that he had nearly always landed the most demanding tasks, the filthiest, worst paid jobs. He would stand at the back, not confident enough to shove to the front like so many others did every morning, and wait for the foreman to get round to him. At first he had been sent back home with the last few stragglers, mainly older men, or sickly looking types who smoked and coughed and spat a lot. But later, once they saw how he uncomplainingly accepted the jobs nobody else was desperate enough to take on, he became a fixture. He was strong, and young and healthy, and that made up for his doziness. For what he was expected to do it was better not to think too much, anyway. Petunia for her part had supplemented his income by cleaning apartment blocks, office blocks, private homes, anything that would give her a wage, no matter how small.

'Today our luck will change,'

she had said. Now Ambrose didn't believe in luck.

He lit another cigarette, a habit he'd picked up behind bars. It was smelly, and would maybe even kill him one day, not that that mattered much now, but it helped calm the nerves and gave him something to look forward to. As he smoked he stared out the bedroom window at the blue, blue sky, and thought of nothing whatsoever, a mental trick that more than one would give a fortune to command. When he had finished he stubbed it out on his heel and popped the butt into his pocket with the others. He had quite a collection by now.

Back downstairs he once again passed by the service dining room. They had spent many a long evening here, eating and drinking and laughing with Señora Luz and Brendan and Stein, but it was the memory of Mrs Haute, white as a ghost, that came back to him now.

They had cleared away the evening meal and were sitting around, as usual, having a nightcap, camomile for the ladies, brandy for the men, the final ritual before they each went off to their private rooms. Maybe they'd been watching TV, or perhaps there had been conversation, no doubt about recent sports events, or the next day's menu, or an anecdote of some kind, any topic that could be trusted to steer well clear of politics, religion or sexual preferences. They had all been together for years now, and the pecking order had not only been established, it had become so intimately understood, so comfortable to live with, that it was virtually adored. Ambrose couldn't remember the exact details now, but he would never forget the way she had wandered in as if she had mislaid something. No, more like she'd taken an overdose, or drunk too much sherry. All this was extremely strange, as Mrs. Haute rarely if ever visited them in the staff quarters, and never unannounced. Pet told him later that she had felt it as soon as the poor woman had entered. They fell silent as soon as they realised who it was, and waited for the lady of the house to speak. Still dressed in her overcoat she had gazed at the ceiling as she had said in a rehearsed voice

'Sydney has had a terrible accident. Tonight, at around nine thirty. He was rushed to hospital where doctors.... could do nothing.... to reanimate him. I'm sorry.'

She had left in a hurry before the staff could muster up so much as a 'my condolences'. Pet had started crying then, with huge, uncontrollable sobs, and could not stop despite Brendan's stunned support. Luz had rushed out after her mistress, but had soon come back, wringing her hands, unable to enter the lady's room. Stein and Ambrose had stared at their plates in shock, their worlds on pause.

Sydney was dead, then. He had been thrown from his car straight into a tree. It hadn't made much sense. Not even thirty. He had been so healthy and intelligent, too strong and bright to just die. And his wife Andrea five months pregnant! And Petunia sobbing uncontrollably. What a night.

'It's never going to be the same here again,'

Pet had stated in a dramatic voice. He had been warned.

The double doors that led to the Haute part of the house were also locked, which was something he had not foreseen. He pulled at them vigorously, but they held firm, so he went back into the kitchen for a knife. He needed one that was thin enough to enter the crack between the doors, but strong enough to lever them open. He ended up choosing the largest of them all, a cleaver of sorts, but less bulky. It took some time, but he eventually managed to force the double doors open and accede to the main part of the mansion. He left the cleaver on a thin two legged table that sat against the wall, and headed towards the main entrance hall.

Sydney Haute had been cut down in his prime, and that had convinced Petunia that Life, Life in general, is capricious and spiteful. He was the only son and heir of Arnold Haute, in his turn son of the great Randolph Haute, who had made a fortune out of ball bearings of all things. Had that caught George Ork's attention, Ambrose would now be known as Randy. Sydney, as most people had pointed out, had not lived up to one of the versions of his family name, was anything but haughty. He had been a genuinely friendly type, cheerful, bright, and understandably happy with his lot. Life in general had bestowed him with its finest honours, the sun had shone on his whole existence. His life had ended instantly on collision with a tree by the side of a country road. Now after his name came two dates in brackets, and he was no more.

Attention to detail. He had to pay attention to detail and follow the plan to the letter, foresee anything that could go wrong or change things. One of these was to check the mail. Ambrose had not understood why, it certainly didn't seem important. After all, it wasn't *his* post. Spotty had explained.

'It's to cut out unforseenables. Improbabilities that turn probable, right?'

Spotty enjoyed baffling Ambrose.

'Imagine he comes in and there's a letter on the floor'

'They don't fall onto the floor, there's a basket just behind the letter box.'

'Or wherever. A missive, right? But one that's overpoweringly more urgent than the job in hand. What does he do? He scrams, leaving you wondering what went wrong. It's the detail, the devil is in the detail, the devil's tail, right?'

Ambrose didn't doubt it, Spotty was a lot brighter than he was. He opened the basket and took out the mail. Nothing too interesting, they looked like bills mostly, nothing that would make you scram in his opinion, but he tucked them into his back pocket just in case.

He stood for a moment and recapped. The wall, the alarm, the back door, the post. So far so good.

It wasn't part of the plan, at least not part of the plan he had put together in prison with Spotty, but as he had caught the earlier bus and had so much time on his hands, he decided it wouldn't hurt to go upstairs and have a snoop around, for old time's sake.

Totally alone in the grand old mansion he could have taken the main staircase, a hand carved masterpiece sculpted out of dark wood which swung up to the first floor under tapestries and chandelier, but he instinctively headed for the service stairs.

Walking through the rooms on that floor was like being taken on a guided tour of the Haute family tragedy - Mrs. Haute, Sydney and Andrea, the nursery. He pushed open the door to what had been the young couple's room, and gingerly poked his head inside, almost as if he expected the young master of the house to still be sitting at his desk by the window. Sydney had always been kind to Ambrose, had never ridiculed him or called him a buffoon like Harvey had later. Quite the opposite, he had shown great interest in Ambrose's work. 'How's it going, Bro?' he would ask, and always wait and listen to the answer, unlike others. The young master of the house had been so popular, just like one of the family. But Sydney had died, and Petunia had been right – nothing had been the same after that. Andrea had gone on to give to birth to Sydney Jr. and....

Ambrose clenched his teeth. He did not want to think about that again, not just yet.

Mrs Haute's room had hardly been touched since her death. Her personal belongings had been removed and stored in the basement, but the furniture and decorations remained as she had left them. The room was no longer used. The poor woman, 'sparrow' Pet had called her back then, just seemed to deflate like a balloon the day after a party. She probably agreed with Pet that life in general was capricious and spiteful. Her only son, the marvellous, loveable Sydney had just.... She must have felt suddenly so alone, a widow with a dead son to mourn. Being surrounded by wealth and comfort at such a time was particularly ironic, almost sadistic. Her friends gave her a wide berth, which was interpreted by the more compassionate as a desire not to intrude, whilst the more cynical suspected that they were unwilling to allow even the vaguest trace of tragedy to enter their perfectly polished, successful lives in case it was contagious. The birth of her grandson and heir, Sydney Jr., had done nothing to change her spirits, and little by little she had just faded away. She had become perpetually ill, eternally depressed, cloistered in her room as if the world outside had ceased to exist. Perhaps for her it had. She had drifted on like that until one day she had silently flickered out. Ambrose had helped carry her coffin to the mausoleum whilst his sister had looked after young Sydney Jr., still just a toddler.

He could hear Spotty's voice telling him to stick to the plan, to keep an eye on the details, not to get carried away or distracted. He was a good man, Spotty, even if he had killed that insurance man. Ambrose cut off his tour and went to get the shotgun.

2

Harvey Paulson was born at the right time, in the right place. He was also lucky enough to have been born into the right race, the right sex, on the right side of town. And he was as sharp as a knife.

He was like a fully wound up toy, bursting with contained energy. His movements were swift, deft and effective, as if he knew exactly what he wanted at every turn. This morning he was choosing his clothes for the day, picking them off the hangers in the walk-in wardrobe without hesitation then laying them out on the bed for one final appraisal. Unlike his wife Andrea he did not ponder over the minor details for hours at a time, trying on garment after garment in various combinations before reaching a not necessarily conclusive decision. The adequate attire had been thought through in under a minute, with accessories to match - he knew exactly the impression he wanted to give. He glanced at the alarm clock for confirmation. Eight thirty three. As well he knew he was on schedule, time being an element he had learnt to control in his youth. It took him an average of twenty minutes to choose his wardrobe, shower, shave and dress. Therefore he gave himself twenty-five minutes, just in case he needed to sit on the toilet, or change a shirt with a missing button, or solve any other variable. Should anything else go horribly wrong the time could be made up out of the extra five or ten minutes he gave himself for breakfast and getting the car ready. So it was that Harvey Paulson was rarely, if ever, late. It was merely a matter of knowing how long certain tasks took to complete, then following them orderly to their conclusion. This was not rocket science, and was so simple to achieve, that he found others' unpunctuality irritating and unforgivable. It was slovenliness on their part, and showed a lack of interest which could ultimately be conceived as rudeness, a discourteous attitude bordering on insult.

Breakfast he took on the verandah, with its magnificent views of the ocean, under the shade of purple bougainvillea and a beige beach umbrella, as the summer sun could be quite intense even at this early hour of the day. Beach towels hung over the metal railings of the terrace, and a smell of sun tan lotion floating in on the breeze reminded him that, officially, he was on holiday. Except that people like Harvey are hardly ever on holiday. Their minds are like round the clock machinery, nonstop production lines which go on churning out goods while the rest of the world snores on. Even when their bodies are idle, stretched out and oiled on sun beds, or gently bobbing on inflatable mattresses on the blue diamond surface of a pool, their brains keep whirling, processing data, coming up with new ideas that need to be implemented without delay.

He finished his coffee and went back inside, leaving the breakfast things on the glass table for Anne the cleaner to clear up when she arrived at nine. They no longer had live-in staff, not since the incident. Mr. Stein had wisely decided on taking early retirement, and Señora Luz had headed back to where she had originally hailed from, a tiny village up north somewhere, and was now living with her sister's family. They still maintained a minimum contact, birthday greetings and Christmas cards, more out of old world courtesy than any real desire for communication. Nothing else. It was better for all concerned. Nowadays the Paulsons relied on part time staff, home helps and the like, as well as inclusive insurance policies that offered a whole range of plumbers, locksmiths, electricians and other specialised workers. Painters, builders, solar panel installers they contracted if and when necessary. The days of the maintenance man were thankfully gone forever.

The Spanish style villa was tucked away under cork oaks in the more secluded, exclusive part of Kenton Beach. Here the neighbours kept each other at arm's length, surrounded by luxurious gardens full of palms and wisteria. Cascades of fresh, clear water fell into beautiful swimming pools adorned with stone dolphins or mock Grecian columns, sprinklers refreshed the neatly cropped lawns, and from every balcony or garden bench, the ocean, shimmering and shifting like a screensaver. Unfortunately for those who had sought in the resort seclusion and tranquillity, of late Kenton Beach had become famous, and therefore less exclusive. Once a lazy, half forgotten fishing town, untouched by the passing of the years, it had become a Mecca for those who enjoyed exhibiting their good fortune in public. An expensive marina had been built, designed by an award winning firm of architects, attracting the world's wealthy to its notoriously over-priced restaurants and shopping malls. Apartment blocks had sprung up around the waterfront to house the up and coming nouveau riche, the voyeurs, the shoulder rubbers, and when space had finally run out, new developments had spread up the hills until they were dangerously close to the established homes of the early settlers. This physical and economical encroachment was not readily tolerated by the older generation who did not understand this new wave of magnates, capable of flying or sailing halfway round the globe in order to spend their leisure time among hordes of like-minded types. The old school tended to steer well clear of the quayside and its boasting of yachts with armed security guards, its flouting of cars worth more than most of the beach front apartments, its loud, credit card flashing entourages trying to outdo each other in treating money as if it were worthless.

But Harvey loved it. He felt part of the new generation, the classless generation that linked social success solely to the size of their bank statements. There was nothing he enjoyed more than strolling along the promenade admiring the Ferraris and Lamborghinis, bumping into rich acquaintances, comparing notes on the latest tendencies in nautical engineering, wallowing in the lingering scents and designer clothes of his kind of people. Though undoubtedly what he enjoyed above all was being recognised. By guests at the five star hotels, by managers of guide book listed restaurants, by owners of luxury goods. He loved to be pointed out as a lifetime honorary member of the Beach Club, a distinction bestowed to very few, especially in these crowded times. Because this lifestyle was what he had always aspired to, was his natural habitat, was where he belonged. It was with people like this that he could make conversation. They would talk about the only thing they had in common: money. How to make it, how to invest it, how to spend it. How much a person was worth, how much a certain enterprise would return in profit, how much it was wise to squander. It was not idle chat; all of them knew what they were talking about because they had all accumulated more than they could possibly need in five lifetimes. They had worked their way up into the top percentage of humanity, and could now safely compare notes.

He threw a glance up at where Andrea would be sleeping. Best not to bother her, she knew where he was going and it was wiser not to labour the point. He would phone her a little later and argue that he had not wished to disturb her beauty sleep. He tapped his pockets - wallet, keys, agenda.

Harvey had been born to comfort and social success. His father, Arthur Paulson, was a university professor teaching international law to undergraduates most of the year, activity that he supplemented by working as an extremely well paid consultant for large corporations. He had even spent a short term as a government assessor, but had not enjoyed being embroiled in ideological squabbling. As he had been warned before naively accepting the post, 'all is fair in love and war - and politics'. An unassuming, soft mannered man, he had not felt at home with the carry-a-gun-and-be-prepared-to-use-it ruthlessness of the political arena. He preferred chess, a game in which the rules apply to everyone, and where the most astute and visionary player will invariably sweep the board, cornering and ensnaring his rival, but never moving in for the kill. Mrs. Kelly Paulson was a tall, thin, energetic woman who earned an income by writing secondary school biology text books, so it could be said that the only financial difficulty the family had was keeping track of their numerous investments and properties.

Today he would take the four wheel drive, a bit heavy on consumption but better suited to the dusty, rutted approach routes to La Barraca, where he intended to have lunch before pushing on to Langley. He placed his briefcase in the passenger seat, unnecessarily readjusted the mirrors, dropped his sunglasses down from his hair onto his nose, and started her up. Just before nine. Perfect.

Andrea heard the whirring of the automatic gates as they opened, closed, and rolled over in her sheets. They slept in separate rooms, and justify it as they would, she realised it could be taken as a true reflection of their relationship. They were not the kind of couple that curled up with each other at night like kids in a thunderstorm. Neither did they hold hands in public, or kiss in front of strangers, or in any way show their feelings for each other. It was something they had never done, a routine they had naturally fallen into and now accepted as ideal for both of them. Perhaps they both thought they made up for it in other ways, like Harvey's gifts of flowers and perfume, or the way she left him room to move, to take control. Did it imply a lack of real affection? Was it respect or coldness? She blew out the questions like tiny bubbles, then watched as they floated out of the window and burst in the morning light.

Other noises told her Anne the cleaner had arrived. They were the comforting sounds of routine: Anne's key in the door, her bag dumped on the sideboard, her footsteps in the kitchen, the clatter of breakfast things in the sink. Soon she would start to hum, silly songs from old fashioned musicals that would stick in Andrea's head for days. She had better make an appearance.

In Randolph Haute's day the journey from Kenton Beach to Langley had taken an entire day, the old coastal route picking through major cities, small ports and tiny villages, until it eventually rolled exhausted into Chester Drive. Nowadays it was a six hour drive, the two laned motorway often cutting away from the coastline and diving inland to save time. He had allowed for coffee breaks, refills and lunch. If he didn't get a puncture or meet a traffic jam the ride should be relaxing enough. If, however, he was unlucky enough to encounter a setback, he would skip lunch at the Barraca and pick up a sandwich at a filling station. If even that failed, he had a contact number. He tuned in to a classical radio station, not because he was a great fan of the stuff, but because it gave a certain elegance to the movement of the traffic. It was also unobtrusive and allowed him to think unpestered, unlike attention-seeking pop or rock. He went over the figures again in case there was an aspect of the deal that had escaped him.

The day stretched out before her, long and lazy, but Andrea had never had an issue with leisure. She had been groomed to accept it for what it was – a privilege to be cherished or taken for granted depending on her mood. She would invite Helen and Lucia over for lunch, take the motor boat out for a spin, sunbathe in the cove, swim, do her exercises, read fashion mags or best-sellers, drink beautifully presented cocktails... there was always plenty to do, without an obligation in sight. It is true that she sometimes cursed her luck, wanted to scream against the outrageous injustice of events, but she was in good hands and the ongoing treatment had so far been a resounding success. Dwelling on the past was not deemed convenient, would not help her come to terms with herself, it was to be considered a closed book. Her therapists, professionally healthy and happy types who clearly understood everything and had all the answers, did not feel that it was wise to mention that the past is open to interpretation, can be edited, lied about and distorted, with important aspects often being omitted or exaggerated. Or that this retrospective revision will change people's perception of their history and therefore the way they react to it and act upon it. No, on a personal level it was best for the past to be converted into a large, heavy stone to be heaved over the side of

Even so she had her days. A disturbing sequence of R.E.M. for instance, when faces would float up from the depths to persecute and accuse her. Or when a snippet from an otherwise harmless conversation would catch in her throat like a fish bone. Then she would need all the help she could get. But for the most part Andrea drifted on much as she always had done, happy to idle away her hours doing nothing in particular.

As a child her every whim had been satisfied. She had been showered in age-specific merchandise and foodstuffs, her large bedroom stuffed full of all the most expensive toys. Her self-esteem had been boosted endlessly, forever being reminded how pretty and bright she was, how lucky to have been born into such a wonderful family, and she had been allowed to behave more or less as she had liked because that way there were no scenes, no tears, no hard feelings. She had been prepared for her present life conscientiously throughout her childhood, blinkered from a harsher reality of sacrifice and uncertainty that had nothing to do with her, was not her lot. School had been a breeze, she had been taught so many things by some of the finest teachers, although she had retained virtually nothing. Her parents had defended her - she should not be judged on exam results alone, that would be too unfair. University had been fun, except for the studying part, though she had been spared the humiliation of not completing her course by a timely change of plans. Unfortunate, her parents had argued, and such a shame, but we have to prepare ourselves for life's little upsets, and the situation has been extremely well assimilated by Andrea given the circumstances. Such was their daughter.

Now her father was dead. A heart attack had carried him off, despite daily pills, by-passes and pacemakers, one Sunday afternoon when she was twenty-two. She had been at a friend's house at the time, and had only been given the news on her return, more than a little drunk and still high on half an ecstasy she had shared with Aylissa. The surgeon has died at home, she remembered thinking, as if there were something terribly ironic, even tragic, about that. 'Mother' had been distraught, rushing around and swearing as if her husband had played some nasty, unforgivable trick on her by just popping off without so much as a goodbye, leaving her to sort out the mess. Typical of him. Two years later she had remarried a jet setting hotel owner who tirelessly flew her all over the globe, which was a godsend as it gave both her and Andrea the perfect excuse to see as little of each other as possible.

She pulled her long, dark hair back into a pony tail and studied her face for imperfections. Her reflection revealed a not unattractive woman, with a determined look, especially round the mouth, but with an air of sadness too, due to her slightly drooping eyebrows which had always made her look forlorn, someone to be pitied. Then she put on her bikini, covered herself in a kind of sarong, and went to greet Anne for breakfast as Harvey pulled in to Galbury for petrol and a coffee. He would phone her from there.

Harvey too was used to getting what he wanted. Most of the time he simply had to desire something for it to fall into his hands like a ripe fruit, but if necessary he would go to any measure to obtain the object of his fancy. As a boy that had meant tantrums, pretence, lies. His parents had lived in fear of his temper and had done their best to appease the beast they had unwittingly created, their pet Frankenstein. The word 'no' could send him into a rage, 'not just now' would lead to hours of sulkiness, 'don't do that' always spelt tears. As he matured so did his repertoire. He learnt how to cajole, how to ingratiate himself. He became the master of subtle threat, sycophantic agreement, feigned nonchalance. Armed with such powerful tools, and an unhealthy amount of tenacity, he virtually always achieved what he proposed.

Sydney Haute's death had genuinely shocked him. The Haute family was one of the oldest and most respected families in the area, and although Harvey had never been a close friend to Sydney, he had met him on numerous occasions, shaken his hand, admired his vintage cars. That he should have lost his life in such an absurd way had irritated Harvey, had made him feel both gloomy and short-tempered, though he could not say why. Apparently the funeral had been discreet and private. Harvey's re-insurance company had sent condolences. Matter closed. Life goes on.

Until one dark, rainy evening in November, at the Rajah, when Harvey had been entertaining some of his office staff as part of an incentive programme, and Andrea had entered the select restaurant with two of her friends. Harvey had watched her through the leaves of palms or reflected in Indian mirrors, how she would let down her hair only to deftly roll it up again into a pony tail, or a bun, or a halfway house effect, exposing her suntanned nape, her perfect, delicate ears. He had stared and stared, but she had remained totally oblivious to his interest, and that had attracted him even more. Finally she had left, and he'd found out from the head waiter that she was none other than Andrea Haute, not only to Harvey's eyes tremendously desirable, but a wealthy widow, Sydney's widow, heiress to one of the largest fortunes ever amassed on those shores. He decided it there and then – she would be his.

The phone rang, so Anne slid off towards the living room.

'Harvey?'

'You're up.'

'Hmm. Having breakfast.'

'Didn't want to wake you. Did I?'

'No. Where are you?'

'Galbury Services. Just for some petrol and a quick coffee. Should be ok, pretty much on schedule.'

There was a short silence. Andrea said nothing, so Harvey

signed off.

'I'll lunch at La Barraca if all goes as planned, then on ..... from there. Back by mid afternoon tomorrow. Phone me if you need me, o.k.?'

'O.k.'

And he hung up. He didn't like talking to Andrea on the phone, she always sounded curt, almost rude. She could do with a course in customer service, he thought, like the one he sent his staff on. He imagined her examining her nails or pulling faces as he spoke. Compare that to the tact and diplomacy he employed so as not to injure her sensibility. He had deliberately avoided asking 'how did you sleep?', because it was a Pandora's box question best avoided. He replaced it with fact. You're up. Then the charitable lie about not wanting to wake her up, sidestepping the fact that he had been dying to hit the road, get out of that idle holiday home, do something that wasn't lolling around pools pretending to be relaxed, as if the months spent there were a well-earned break from their stressful lives in the city. But the worst of it all was how he had to avoid mentioning Haute House, his destination. After all these years she still had to be treated like a child on this issue, as if they were characters in an old melodrama where they would say 'we don't mention... *that...* any more'. Harvey had no time for such sentimentality, for Harvey the past was dust and dry bone. No good could come from reminiscence or regret. Plans and projects belonged to the future, action to the present. The rest was gone forever, to be forgotten as soon as possible. Still, he had phoned her, fulfilled his obligation, concluded the nicety, now he could get on with making some money.

Andrea felt herself slipping, she recognised the symptoms. There was a kind of high-pitched buzzing sound in her ears that only she could discern, coupled with a vague dizziness, a subtle impairment of vision. It was the past moving in its sleep. She would have to tread lightly and make as little noise as possible, busy herself with trivia until it repositioned itself and fell back into heavy slumber. And Harvey was the cause, Harvey and his damned deals, Harvey and his unquenchable thirst for wealth, Harvey and his infatuation with that place that called to him like a siren. She heard her memories groan as they rolled over, so called for Anne to keep her company. If she made herself invisible they would sleep on. She had it on doctor's orders - they should not be disturbed.

Canadian Anne was such excellent therapy for Andrea that she could almost have been prescribed. Her mother had died of cancer when she was twelve, leaving her in the hands, literally, of her drunken father who abused her until she ran away. At seventeen she fell in love with a married man who gave her nothing more than torment and her only child, a dull-eyed boy now eleven years old. She was plump, plain, covered in freckles and moles which meant she could never sit in direct sunlight, and diabetic. Yet she sang merrily at the top of her voice like a modern day Cinderella. She never passed judgement or criticised, rarely complained, and accepted her past as if it were a cheque in her name, something personal and non-transferable. Just as a walk through the oncology department will blow away vanity and self pity, so it was that when Andrea began to sink, Anne provided the perfect lifeline. Now she needed her to talk incessantly about her neighbours, her son, food prices and TV gossip, anything to keep from waking the dead.

La Barraca restaurant, specialising in Spanish cuisine though not closed to other tastes, had been chosen by Harvey not only because it was almost half way on the way to Langley, but because it was safe – Sydney had never been there with Andrea. He had soon found out that the country was like an old map, stained with hotels, concert halls, and beauty spots that had been visited by the happy couple, and which were now taboo. At first he had made the mistake of rebelling against this, of deliberately proposing venues that he knew were strictly out of bounds, hoping that by so doing he could shake her out of her absurd attitude, the way some parents try to teach their children to swim by tossing them in the deep end and leaving them to thrash it out alone. He had obtained V.I.P. seats for the ante penultimate final farewell concert of one of her favourite bands, an extravaganza with lasers and symphony orchestra, only to be told, minutes after he had sprung the surprise on her, that the lady was not for turning. That had been a critical moment in their relationship and had almost led to a rupture. He could not believe that she would have the nerve, the bloody-mindedness, to refuse him. Those tickets had cost him a fortune, it was a fucking surprise, damn you! She clammed up and disappeared into her room. He went alone, and spent the best part of the tedious affair in the lounge bar. Nothing could make her change her mind, Andrea always refused to co-operate – she must avoid such places for her own good, and asking her to revisit such places when there were so many more was not fair, was verging on cruelty. Could Harvey not understand? Could he not comply to this simple request? Please? It was irritating, and curtailed his freedom. He would never be able to go to Lakeside Gardens with her, or to Morley's, or Camberley Heights.

But Haute House, his destination, was different. It was his now, he was the legitimate owner, and he would visit or stay whenever he pleased, because she had been living there when they had met, had shown him round personally, and had only developed her aversion after the incident. It was not the same at all, and he would stand his ground over that. God knows it had cost him enough, so much effort, perhaps even more than he was prepared to admit, and he was not going to renounce it all now, just because little miss fragile couldn't face the facts and move on.

He would be there around five-thirty, six. The opportunity had arisen and he had snatched it up. That was the way to do business, to prosper, to advance. He was not like his wife, despite their apparent similarities of origin. They both came from the same privileged section of society, both had been well educated and pampered, surrounded by wealth and safety, their futures assured and insured. But Harvey had been taught to devour the world, to go out and hunt down his prey, to rise above the rest, to compete, to strive, to achieve. Ambition was the key word, and the overall idea was to turn life into a ceaseless, ever expanding c.v. which could be handed in with his death certificate. It was a vaguely Protestant notion, a system of merits carefully accumulated and hopefully commutable for benefits in a theoretical after life or nether world yet to be defined in detail. It was a paradox that such an astute man as Harvey, who always claimed he had no time for religion or belief, should agree to sign a document where the fine print is either illegible or under revision. Andrea had not been burdened with such anxieties. Her globe-trotting mother had told her she was to enjoy the ride while she could, that she didn't need to go looking for trouble as it would come on its own (so true!), and that it would all be over too soon as it was. Which was why she was spending her time lying about on beach towels and listening to the top ten, while Harvey was eating tortilla de patatas con jamón serrano on his way to Haute House, his real home, his mansion, to sign a deal worth thousands.

Anne chatted on while Andrea did her best to listen, to follow the long descriptions with interest, to keep track of who said what to whom and why. Eventually she knew Anne would have to really get on with her chores, and then Andrea would rush to the phone for a similar chat with Helen. Then they would all meet for lunch and she should be alright from there on. As long as Harvey didn't phone in again. There was a story about a neighbour of Anne's, a little dog, the neighbour on the other side of the road. Somehow all this was related to where Anne had worked as a hairdresser just before she had left Canada. It was safe ground, and Andrea was sure she'd heard most of it before, but as the details changed and she could never remember exactly what had happened, and as Anne was such a vibrant narrator, she took it all in with a smile. This was the best way to cruise through the morning, and the longer Anne took to tell her tale the better. Everything was as it should have been, and would normally have continued in that fashion quite harmlessly, except that today Anne suddenly slipped up in the middle of her humorous yarn and asked, as if it had just occurred to her, 'Where's Harvey gone?

Haute House was the answer, as Anne discovered just a little too late. She realised her mistake as soon as Andrea changed her expression and waved her off with an 'up north on business somewhere'. The way Andrea's face had clouded over, the way she had spoken as if trying to shake off a pestering fly, the vagueness of her reply, 'up north', it could only mean one place, and she had been careless enough to drag it up. She tried to race ahead as if nothing had happened, tearing into her story with renewed enthusiasm, popping in a joke or too and a swear word in a frantic attempt to swerve clear of that haunted house. But it was too late. Andrea pulled herself to her feet wearily and announced that she would go and lie down in the lounge for bit. Anne suggested that she could maybe keep her company, dust or hoover while they gossiped, but Andrea cut her short with a curt 'see you later', and drifted off. Canadian Anne was worried now. If everything went according to the usual plan, Andrea would end up back in the hands of glossy Gustave, drugged to the eyeballs for a few days, then a week or two of personal therapy. How had she been so foolish? Why had she mentioned Harvey in the first place? That's what came of not thinking about what you say, just letting it all trot off your tongue as if nothing mattered. Now she had unwittingly stirred the demons and poor Andrea would have to fight them off all over again. She decided to phone Helen and Lucia, they would know what was best for her.

However the house that had become to be a symbol of tragedy and sorrow for Andrea was to Harvey like a gold medal, awarded to him for outstanding merit. He had overcome immense difficulties and unscrupulously pushed on until he had achieved his goal. It was his prize, it was the winner's cup he held up with both arms to the packed stadium, it was the justification for all his drastic measures and impossible decisions. It was the mirror of his worth. He had fallen in love with it at once and had sworn, on that very first day, that nothing would stand between him and the ownership of that impressive, imposing property. Andrea had shown him round as if she were a bored estate agent's assistant, limiting herself to reciting a list of the rooms as if it had nothing to do with her at all. Kitchen, morning room, drawing room, billiard room, library.... She had only been living there for around four years, and had obviously not grown attached to it, appeared to prefer to keep it all at arm's length. Or rather, she had grown to distrust it, as if it had in some way been partly to blame for Sydney's death. Either way she had whipped round the place like a tourist guide hoping to get home before hitting the rush hour traffic, hastily opening doors then waltzing off along the corridor, dying to get back downstairs to the few rooms she now occupied overlooking the tennis courts.

But Harvey was overawed. He immediately became infatuated with the Old World magnificence of the mansion, its oak and mahogany panels, its uniquely patterned tiled floors, the towering height of the ceilings and windows. Wherever he looked there was beauty, style, opulence. He marvelled at ingeniously designed door knobs, intricate plasterwork, hand-crafted soft furnishings and priceless works of art. He marvelled at the sheer size of the place, its innumerable rooms, the extensive grounds, the rows of cars in the garage, the whitewashed and immaculate staff quarters. It was like something out of an old black and white film or a romantic novel, it was wealth transformed into heritage, and it was within his reach. He would grasp it and possess it, no matter what the cost.

Andrea crept back upstairs, lowered the blinds, and lay down on her bed to rest. The situation was not new, she knew which pills would help, how to breathe, who to phone for help. She understood that she would now be prey to her memories, which far from sinking forever to the forgetful seabed as promised, would now emerge to taunt her once more, bobbing to the surface like....... She tried to find a sustainable rhythm to her breathing, forced herself to focus on the list of positive emotions she had learnt and relearnt so many times, but she soon realised it would be useless without the pills.

In the bathroom she avoided her reflection, loathe to contemplate her pathetic image, fearful of self reproach. Anne's voice cut through the walls with something about Helen. As long as it was not Harvey phoning in. As long as it was not that again.

She had met Sydney Haute in, of all places, a park in Lugano, Italy. As the full moon rose out of the mountains. No, that was later, as they strolled down to the water's edge. It must have been earlier, before dark, before they closed the main gates to the park. Gary had spotted him. He had been so embarrassed! He was taking his mother for a walk! Mrs. Haute, whose first name was Alice, though nobody ever used it, who thought she was so modern that it was pathetic. She was the widow, the heiress, the mother of a dead son. That role had been played by Alice then, now she was Andrea. She had provoked him with her liberty, a wild young woman with no chaperone, had challenged him with her sexuality, but somehow he had managed to turn the tables and she had found herself following him around like a dog from that moment on. Despite herself. She had loved his smile, his forearms, his lithe movements. Oh, he had been so perfect. Somehow she just knew he had died with a smile on his lips. C'est la vie! C'est la mort! But she was being romantic, allowing her memories to fool her, letting the passing of time do its patronising editing. Of course there had been another side, an alternative truth. She shuddered. Yes, he could be cold too, like his mother, cruelly distant, disdainful.

She was shown an image of him entering without so much as a glance in her direction, all his attributes turned suddenly into ugliness through that indifferent gesture. It is so strange how liquid love hardens into icy routine. How the torrid passion of hotel rooms cools into... into... whatever.

Whatever, she repeated, hoping to thwart the return of that first floor bedroom with its inherited furniture impregnated with the souls of long dead aunts or the unknown daughters of rich businessmen, who had combed their beautiful locks in the self same mirrors of the dressing table that needed so much care but could not be removed or replaced or put into doubt for one instant without Alice Haute frowning and tut-tutting at dear, obedient Sydney, the protector of the Family Legend. The furniture stays put. The wardrobe is too small, but it will have to do. The basin is ancient and noisy, but it is not to be touched. The room is cold, and draughty, with its own personality, and I hate it. Hate House.

As the pill at last began to do its job of numbing Andrea into semi consciousness, Harvey checked his phone and his watch. Bang on schedule and no hitches in sight. Soon he would pull up before the wrought iron gates and the double H would part and swing open, revealing his estate, his achievement. The idea was to get there a full half hour before the film boys turned up, get the cars out onto the forecourt and warm them up a little, get them purring. He had told Brendan Jr. to wash and wax them so that they would shine in the evening light as they deserved to shine. That should impress them if they had any idea what they were talking about.

He had to congratulate Sydney and his forebears for the collection. Here were cars made for kings and magnates, mythical vehicles that archdukes would be proud to be assassinated in, cars fit for a triumphal drive through conquered European capital cities, roadsters from which Hollywood filmstars could fly to premature deaths, to celluloid immortality. They were unique, with an air of eccentricity, and all beautifully maintained by Mint Condition, a local firm of enthusiasts and retired mechanics that specialized in vintage cars. Perfectly roadworthy, with all their papers in order, they were irreplaceable. At first he had not been able to memorise their names and numbers, but by now they sounded like the names of friends or family. Amongst others there was the extravagant 1931 Lancia Dilambda with Viotti coachwork, a cream and tan work of art which had appeared in films before Harvey had even met Andrea. The black 1935 Duesenberg SJN, ready to pounce, its thin windshield like narrowed eyes. The red 1947 Buick Super with its Botero lines, and, Sydney's favourite, an olive green 1938 SS100 Jaguar racing car. Superb beasts suitable for only the most exquisite owners.

He had rented the Jaguar out before, again to a film company, and had struck a hard deal. He knew its worth, especially in tip top condition. Now they wanted the lot. They would have to be prepared to pay for it, and so far they seemed more than willing. He would demand additional insurance too, it would give him more bargaining power.

He turned off the classical music; the racing up and down of scales was beginning to irritate him. Music to him was something to accompany a feeling, an ambience. It was nothing in itself, and out of context could even send him into a fit of anger. The nonsense Andrea listened to at full blast in the kitchen as she played at being a housewife, sporting an apron and a glass of white wine, putting onto plates food that Anne had no doubt prepared the day before, would fill him with rage, making him turn it off with a brusque gesture, swearing it made him unable to think. She would suggest then that he find another room, or stop thinking, and turn it back on. She was not afraid of Harvey and his tantrums, and could play that game all day if he wished. You turn it off, I'll turn it back on, hour after hour. She was as stubborn as he was if put to the test. Finally he would leave, muttering 'women!' under his breath, hoping by that to convey to Andrea that the incident could not be understood as a minor victory on her part, but rather a gracious retreat on his. She did not even consider it. Now he drove on in silence as she drifted off into the arms of her narcotic protector.

Andrea lay drugged on her bed like a valuable jewel kept in a velvet-lined box. Despite her promising start in life, despite her birth right, life had not turned out as she had imagined. At school, in her language class, she had learnt about the if-clause, the third conditional as they had called it, an abstract idea that had not fired her imagination at the time. It was a grammatical term for dealing with the impossible, the hypothetical, she had been told. If. If she had not met Sydney. If she had not gone down to the park that day with the gang, but stayed in the hotel reading or listening to music. If she had not met Harvey. Or rather, if Harvey had not noticed her in that Indian restaurant and pestered her for a date. If she had only….. Pure speculation. Things could have been different, but they weren't, and there was little or no point in dwelling on impossibilities. Smooth talking Gustave knew that, they all knew that. It was lesson one, or at least part of it. But it was also very difficult to avoid, this rewriting of the past, this reinvention of a life. If her father had not died, if she had not gone to Italy but to Istanbul, if she had had the foresight or the strength to resist Harvey's advances, his ambition, his…... No, that was something she would not say, something she refused to accept or admit. That would be too much, far too much. The whims of fate could just about be tolerated, as long as it was all down to chance, to abstract third conditionals. If that was the case she would manage to carry on. The alternative, the idea that there had been some kind of interference, that the course of events had been deliberately manipulated, she would not be able to cope with, could not possibly live with. Such notions had to be driven out of her, or killed off by drugs and therapy. She was better off in her comfortable cocoon, safe and unaware.

As for Harvey, soon he would arrive at Haute House, at the destiny he had forged for himself over the years with so much tenacity and cunning. All his natural intelligence, all his innate strength of will and character, everything he had gained or learnt over the years, everything, had been used to achieve this marvellous symbol of power and wealth. And now that Andrea refused to even mention the place, it was, at last, all his.

3

Later the police would try to create a reconstruction of the incident, laying out things just as they had been on that unforgettable day, forcing people to re-enact their moves to the minute and the metre, positioning and timing their movements as in an over rehearsed play. They hoped that this piece of memorised theatre, along with the rest of their investigations, would give them an indication as to what really happened, who was to blame, if there were some obscure and hidden motive, who could be eliminated from their suspicions. But it was never going to be easy. Some apparently significant evidence turned out later to be no more than a red herring, and other valuable clues were missed in a deluge of minor detail. To really understand what took place that day they would need to spend long stretches of time at Haute House, living with the protagonists, interviewing and cross-examining them over and over again. That would not be possible, that belonged to the realm of the third conditional. So they would have to reach their conclusions like all of us, by picking through the information at hand.

How much information needs to be collected? How far back in time do we have to go to find the answers that help us understand a tragedy? Reasonable questions, but a police investigation cannot waste time on such philosophical niceties, it must be practical. They decided to start from when Harvey Paulson first became part of life at Haute House.

First impressions count, especially to the astute. A shrewd person with experience and an eye for detail is able to pigeon-hole a new acquaintance within minutes. A scan is run and the results analysed. Carefully interpreted, this data should define social class, as relayed through clothing and accessories, as well as any number of clues about that person's habits. Do they practice sport, overeat, ever visit the dentist? A deeper scan seeks out more subtle traits. Are they submissive, arrogant, challenging? Taken one step further, many people will dress and present themselves in a studied manner to deliberately create the desired impression. That way they are telling their audience not necessarily who they are, but more who they would like to be, who they are prepared to be. Which was why Pet had made Ambrose wear his Sunday best for the interview with Stein and Mrs Haute that hot August day. Nobody would really believe they felt comfortable dressed that way, Petunia in a frock she had worn to a wedding, Ambrose in a suit fit for other seasons, but at least they would give the impression of being willing to make the effort, to show respect, to behave themselves and try to blend in. Mr. Stein had been amused, Mrs. Haute had been pleased. If Ambrose had gone in his jeans and his favourite cartoon character T-shirt who knows what would have become of them?

Today it was her turn. Andrea would soon turn up with her new man, Harvey Paulson, who she had been dating for the last few months, and Pet would have the opportunity to size him up. There were mixed feelings in the household about this new affair of Andrea's. Most agreed that after almost three years of grieving the fact that she had decided to start a new relationship was positive, a healthy sign that suggested that she had finally laid Sydney, and consequently Mrs. Haute, to rest. She needed to snap out of her lethargy, of her doting on little Sydney Jr,, because she was still young and attractive and had her whole life ahead of her. And what a life! As mother of the only heir to Haute House she would hold the reins of the estate until the young man's coming of age. The late Mrs. Haute had left everything to her only grandson, to be inherited once the boy became a man, at eighteen. She would have preferred twenty one, but her lawyer had persuaded her to move with the times. In the meantime, the economic affairs would be run by a group of advisors named specifically for the task by Alice Haute just before her death. Andrea was to receive a generous annual income and use of both Haute House and the villa at Kenton Beach for the rest of her days. So without having to worry her pretty little head about a thing, she was to lead a life of luxury and leisure for which she had been perfectly prepared.

The problem was she was now all alone. True, she had her son, a carbon copy of the father he had never seen, but the boy was still in nappies and more of a burden than company. Andrea was not a natural mother, did not possess a very strong maternal instinct, and expected her child to be brought up with the help of others, saving for herself the beautiful moments of giggles and cuddles, whilst delegating the more tedious tasks to the staff, which basically meant Pet. So she had too much time to ponder on her bad luck, on her loss, on her unsought though fabulous inheritance. What she needed, her friends and relatives all agreed, was an adventure. And by all accounts that moment had arrived in the form of Harvey Paulson.

But who was this Harvey? Could he hope to match Sydney's magnificent memory? Would Sydney Jr. take to him? Was it wise to invite him here, to the House, so soon? The staff felt protective towards Andrea, wanted to save her from any kind of deception, to keep her safe from fortune hunters and unscrupulous Casanovas. Not so much for her; she was a relative newcomer to the place, and although was well liked, she had not been in their lives long enough to be loved. She was to be pitied though, for she had suffered so much. Their real concern was for Sydney Jr., the fatherless, fair-headed toddler who ran riot throughout the mansion totally oblivious to the blows and machinations of his inherited world. Would this Harvey Paulson treat him well, be a good father to the boy? They were about to find out.

Ambrose would be present on Harvey's arrival too, but he would have to leave the appraisals to his sister; he was useless at that kind of thing. It was a knack he had never learnt, and he was not even truly convinced of the science behind it all. It seemed to him that mistakes had been made on more than one occasion. Hadn't they found the Wiggins to be charming? Hadn't Pet even said that she found Mr. Golden Nugget Cummings to be a perfect gentleman? And he remembered that you should never judge a book by its cover. His parents had told him that. And his teachers. In fact just about everybody knew that, even if they chose to ignore it. But she assured him that she knew better, so he supposed she probably did, she usually did. He half wondered for a moment about why people would talk about judging covers and so on, but never pay the slightest bit of attention to it. Maybe there was something he was missing. He let it drop. The best thing to do was to start with a friendly greeting, and then wait for a report later on in the day when his sister had decided that she'd seen enough to reach a reasonable conclusion.

'He'll be here for lunch. I've put your clean clothes on your bed, so when you've finished with the bins, have a quick shower and get dressed, alright? Be ready by twelve at the latest. Alright? Twelve o'clock. At the latest. They're on your bed. Ah, and change your boots, too, don't forget, ok?'

Pet invariably spoke to Ambrose as if she were his mother, it was something she had always done, an attitude she had subconsciously taken towards him even long before their mother had died. Ambrose didn't mind; he was used to it. Anyway, she was his big sister and she knew best.

She hadn't mentioned anything to him, but Ambrose could see that Pet was not entirely convinced about the lunchtime visit. She was not her usual chirpy self, was a bit serious, and frowned as she turned away. More than once she studied the sky, watching the passing clouds closely and shaking her head. Signs, he supposed, signs only Pet could interpret. Was there anything in it? Was it like crossing your fingers, and black cats and the like? Or could his sister judge the world by its cover? Either way he trusted her, knew he could always rely on her better judgement. Hadn't she been the one who had got them the jobs in the first place?

Though it had to be admitted that the Haute House that Harvey was about to discover bore little resemblance now to the family home that had taken them on so many years back. Those were the days when Sydney was in his prime and Mrs. Alice Haute ruled the roost with cool glamour, with studied charm, so very old fashioned despite her modern ways. If poor, dead Sydney had judged books by their covers he certainly hadn't shown it. From the very first day he had been both polite and amiable, showing a genuine interest without the vaguest trace of mockery. He had called Petunia Pet, and Ambrose Bro, because he realised that they would appreciate it, would understand that he was being affectionate, not rude. When Mr. Stein bawled at Ambrose, he would wink conspiratorially and say things like 'don't be too hard on him, Mr. Stein!' (Mr. Stein would not expect to be called 'Joe' whilst in his official role). One day he helped Pet clear away the breakfast things, chatting about this and that and laughing at her cheeky comments. Never once did he mention her weight, or her smoking habit, or her dental hygiene. And there was the time he took off his jacket and pushed the old Volkswagen right up the drive and round the back to the garages. He didn't even call for Ambrose to give him a hand, just did it all on his own, one hand on the wheel, the other pushing hard, his feet digging into the gravel, until he had it where he wanted it. When Mr. Stein had complained and tried to blame Ambrose for being lazy and inconsiderate, Sydney had just laughed and patted Ambrose on the back. 'Exercise is good for you' he had said, and thrown a smile at both of them.

Then Andrea had come along, and had been accepted immediately by both family and staff. If Sydney was the perfect, well-educated son, then Andrea would be his perfect match. She too was well-educated and polite, was comfortable with wealth and its exigencies, knew how to behave and belong. The presence of cooks and cleaners did not disturb her in any way; she had been groomed for a life of leisure and knew her part. So she was approachable though respected, which was the ideal balance that Alice Haute had been looking for in a daughter-in-law. She also had a pleasant, unruffled character which made cohabitation a remarkably non-traumatic affair.

Then life had turned capricious. Sydney, the envy of the county, was hurled into a tree at speed and killed instantly. Mrs. Alice Haute died as a result of that accident, too. And Andrea was left to fend for herself and her new born son surrounded by the belongings and memories of the dead.

Andrea had not wanted a reception party. She imagined the servants, the staff, lined up on the steps of the entrance waiting for the carriage to arrive, butlers and maids all dressed in full uniform, humble and grateful, as in days of yore or in historical films. No, she was a woman of her times, modern and relaxed, so there would be no standing on ceremony. She would simply turn up at an unspecified time and have a light lunch in her rooms with her new acquaintance. She had no intention of introducing Harvey to them as if he were an official suitor; it was her business, not theirs. So the staff decided to work out their own choreography; all of them would appear naturally whilst carrying out their daily tasks, and by pure chance manage to be in the right place at the right time. Nobody wanted to miss the opportunity to get a good long look at this Harvey Paulson who seemed to be making such an impression on Andrea. Because it had escaped no-one's attention that just recently Andrea had become, if not happier, then at least less depressed. She smiled more often, played more with Sydney Jr. and took more care of her hair and clothes. For those reasons alone Harvey was to be received without animosity; they would give him a fair chance to prove his worth. Not that they would ever have a say in the matter or be consulted in any way. They were paid to supply service, not to act as a kind of proxy family. But maybe if Andrea noticed their enthusiasm, or caution, or aversion, she would think twice before taking any decision she may later regret. They all liked to think they had some kind of influence over what took place at Haute House, though since Sydney's and his mother's deaths their powers of persuasion had dwindled. Andrea was now in charge, a relative newcomer, and for the past two years she had lived in virtual reclusion, occupying only half a wing of the ground floor, as if the rest of the house belonged to those who cleaned and maintained it. The real decisions were made off premises by the advisors appointed in their day by Alice Haute. Nonetheless they saw it as their duty; Harvey would be assessed, and the results would be written all over their faces.

'It was at 12.09 on Thursday the seventeenth of March. I'll never forget.'

Pet had a prodigious memory. She could tell you exactly when Sydney had died, when Mrs. Haute had passed away. She knew the wedding dates and birthdays and even the saint's days of almost everyone she had ever met. So there was no doubt about it – Harvey had arrived that day at 12.09.

As an accessory a car can be a very potent calling card. A lot is said about a person who turns up in a Porsche, or a two-seater of any kind. First and foremost it means No Kids. Alternatively a large sedan car, in sombre dark grey, powerful yet discreet, denotes responsibility and decency. An orange Beetle with racing stripes tells another story. So they waited expectantly to find out what type of vehicle Harvey drove. Brendan would be first to spot it, as he had positioned himself near the main gates. He watched anxiously as possible candidates approached, only to drive past. He saw an Audi, white and sleek, dither as if unsure which way to turn, but as it crawled past he noticed the woman driver was well into her sixties. A four by four Toyota? No, that was Joe Higgins' car. A black Ford van he thought was unlikely, but worth tracking nonetheless. It parked a little further up the street. Nobody got out, at least not while he was watching.

Eventually a taxi pulled up at the gates, and a short, stout young man with dark hair and casual clothes alighted. He opened the back door for Andrea, then paid the taxi, which pulled away noiselessly. He was no fool this Harvey, he would keep them guessing.

They entered the grounds through a side gate and walked up the drive to the main door. They did not hold hands, they did not talk. Andrea, clad entirely in denim, led the way with her lazy, loping gait, while Harvey, keen and alert in khaki and navy blue, took in the sight. Brendan, who had taken the opportunity to wish them good day, slipped off to find the rest.

When the couple entered the house, they were met by Mr. Stein and Señora Luz, who just happened to be going over a few unspecific minor arrangements. They were duly introduced to the guest. On the way to Andrea's quarters they almost literally bumped into Petunia, who was carrying some plastic bags on her way to the kitchen. Andrea nodded, Harvey smiled politely, and they were gone. Not much of an encounter, but she had seen enough. She watched as they disappeared into Andrea's rooms.

Ambrose was still getting dressed. He had found an old pair of sunglasses in a kitchen drawer and was trying to decide if he should wear them or not. He liked to think that they were rather stylish, and made him look attractive, but it was hard to know for sure. More than once Pet had ridiculed his dress sense, swearing he had no taste. Which is why she chose his wardrobe, even his accessories. She even took it upon herself to help him choose what tattoo he should have, and where it should go. His hairdresser was a friend of hers and styled Ambrose as Pet saw fit, moving with the fashion that most impressed her at the time. So he rarely wore anything that his sister hadn't bought for him or previously approved. Every so often he would try to put his foot down and insist on a certain cap, or a pair of shorts, but Pet could always cajole him out of his obstinacy. Still, the sunglasses he thought she might just agree to.

Pet rushed into the room.

'He's here. I've just seen him downstairs. What are you doing?'

Ambrose struck a pose and winked, unaware that she could not see his eyes through the dark lenses of his shades.

'For Pete's sake take them off. Where did you get them? You look ridiculous. Come on, we have to go down and see if we can spot them again. She's bound to show him round at one point.'

Ambrose slipped the sunglasses into his pocket and followed his sister obediently.

The staff took up positions and continued their surveillance. Brendan would keep an eye on the small terrace in case the sun came out and they should decide to take a stroll through the grounds via the French windows. Stein and Luz would alternate along the main corridor. Pet and Ambrose would hover round the games room area which was connected to Andrea's rooms by a not very often used side door. Still, better be on the safe side. The moment the couple appeared, the staff would accidently place themselves in a position from where they could get a better view of the young pretender.

Harvey realized this and was on his best behaviour. He knew how to hold himself on such occasions, knew how to charm and delight. His aim was for all those who met him to think that he was 'nice'. His parents and his upbringing had given him all the advice necessary to succeed in society, even if he did choose to ignore it some of the time, and today those lessons would be put into practice. So he feigned interest, was courteous, made an effort to smile, pretended to be shy and a little out of place in such magnificent surroundings. Therefore he was grateful to the staff for their consideration. That day Harvey Paulson was a perfect gentleman.

He eventually met Ambrose in the hall as he was about to leave. He noticed that the man seemed to be more than a little embarrassed, unsure whether to grin or remain straight-faced. Ambrose, (was that his name? his real name?) shuffled his feet, and his mouth hung open at intervals. He looked as if he were about to go to Sunday school, and kept toying with something in his pocket all the time. He thought: the man's a fool. But Harvey nonetheless smiled and bowed his head, said that he was pleased to make his acquaintance, and sauntered off to the main gates where his taxi awaited him. Pet had witnessed the whole scene.

She had also been present when young Sydney had been brought down from his afternoon nap to meet his future step-father. This Harvey character had gone through the motions, but he wasn't fooling her; she had all the information she needed.

That had been the most difficult encounter for Harvey. Sydney Jr. was like a miniature, cherubic version of Sydney Haute, deceased, thereby reminding Harvey that this was still very much the home of the Haute family. The outsider, the newcomer, the upstart even, was Harvey Paulson. This little boy, with his unsought inheritance, was inadvertently underlining the fact that, for the time being, Harvey was no more than a visitor. Not even the widow held the keys to the treasure; it all resided in that small child. Which, added to the fact that Harvey had never had any time for children, made petting the boy an act of determination, of self-sacrifice. Not only was Sydney Jr. a noisy, uncontrollable, whining nuisance, he was another man's offspring, a competitor for Andrea's affection, and an obstacle placed between himself and control of the Haute fortune. Not the best credentials for establishing a relationship. Still, appearances were everything, especially on first encounters, so Harvey had done what anyone would have done. He ruffled the boy's hair, asked his age (two fingers for an answer), and gave him a bag of sweets. That was enough for one day; he left Andrea in charge after that.

In the taxi on his way back to town Harvey decided his fate; he would make Andrea his wife and take charge of affairs at Haute

House.

Over supper in the kitchen, the TV on for background noise, the topic of conversation was Harvey. They discussed his looks, his attitude, his background, his chances, his intentions. The general opinion was that he seemed to be a 'nice enough' man. Well-dressed but not over-dressed. Correct but not too distant, nor too informal. That he came from a decent family went without saying, his manner and bearing could testify to that. A bit short, maybe. That was Joe Stein, though he himself was not exactly tall. When Andrea put on her high heels she'd be a good bit taller. They nodded; height could be a problem. Unless he wore platform boots, suggested Ambrose. They all laughed except Pet, who had so far held her tongue.

'Well, you'd better get used to him, 'cos he's here to stay.'

'The lady has spoken,'

jibed Mr. Stein.

'Not your type, Pet?'

Inquired Brendan, winking at Ambrose.

'I don't like him, not one little bit. There's something shifty about him, something, I don't know, something not right. He gives me the creeps.'

'I don't think we should leap to conclusions, we hardly know the man,'

said Luz, almost as a rebuke.

'He seemed nice enough to me,'

added Joe Stein.

Pet fell silent. Ambrose looked at each of them in turn, and understood nothing. They couldn't all be right about Harvey, but who to trust? He very much respected Joe Stein. Here was a man who could do almost anything, from fixing a car to rebooting a computer, a man of letters and figures, a man with a cool head and a keen eye. And Luz was no fool, with her photographic memory and an internal clock that worked to the minute. Brendan Senior was his friend, he was old and wise, and he had clearly stated earlier in the conversation that the new man had come across as alright. So that meant Pet was the only one who did not agree, had seen something the others hadn't. But she did have that power, he knew. Apart from the Wiggins she had nearly always been right. He was unsure how she managed it, there were candles and numbers and weather patterns involved, and it was all too mysterious for him to grasp. But she really did have hunches, and they really did work most of the time, so what was the verdict? Was Harvey ok, harmless enough, a chap to be trusted? Or was he to be feared? Was it best to tread carefully in his presence? Or would it all come to nothing anyway? A brief passion with no future? And why couldn't they ever *agree* to anything? Why did they all talk and talk and never reach a joint conclusion? Why did it all have to be so damned difficult? Maybe he should try another joke, like the one about the platform shoes. He shot a glance at his sister who was picking at her potatoes sullenly. Maybe not, he decided.

'Either way, it'll do her the world of good; it'll take her mind off everything and… do her the world of good.'

Mr. Stein's words were to be taken as final. It was not Pet's place now to contradict him, so she let it go and bent with the conversational wind.

She was right about one thing – Harvey had come to stay. He had discovered that Andrea pined to be treated like a princess, to be showered in gifts and unexpected treats, to be adored and admired. So he sent roses, dozens of them, by private courier. It was not cheap, but it was easy and effective. At the swipe of a credit card he had her enthralled, delighted that the old world clichéd charm of being surrounded by red rose buds should at last be hers. Because Harvey had soon realized that he needed to fill the gaps that Sydney had failed to attend to, and being romantic was definitely the fastest route to goal. Personally he considered it to be sickly sweet, pathetic, infantile, puerile, and something that he hoped she would eventually grow out of. He had once dated a girl whose room was a display of soft toys and dolls, many of them still in their plastic coverings to keep the dust off them, not the most erotic setting. But for the time being playing the game was what Andrea required of him, what distanced him from his predecessor. Sydney had made her laugh, had overawed her, had managed to turn her to jelly in his presence. She had fallen in love with him to such a degree that, looking back, it now appeared as if their love had been a lop-sided affair. She had been infatuated by his persona, inebriated by his carefree nonchalance and joie de vie, had all but worshipped the man. She did not want that to happen again. If she were to start afresh, she wanted to be pampered, if she were to love again, she wanted to be loved back, if she were to let Harvey into her life, he would have to be both the perfect gentleman and an ardent fan of everything that was Andrea. He could begin by sending roses.

So it was that Harvey Paulson became a fixture at the Haute household, arriving at all hours, invariably bearing gifts, courteous and attentive. His attentions were obsessively turned on Andrea, and she was so overwhelmed by this show of devotion and affection that she did not realize that Harvey was never any more than correct towards young Sydney. He only has eyes for his love, she assumed, and thought no more of it. She was being swept off her feet and enjoying every moment of it. After so much suffering, after such a long winter, she believed she was entitled to a little happiness.

But Pet had noticed it, how Harvey kept the child at bay with sweets, how he could not bring himself to cuddle the boy, or pick him up and carry him in his arms. He patted him on the head and then waited for someone to intervene, to lead him off to his toys, or upstairs for a siesta, or to the kitchen for his lunch. If Sydney started to pester Harvey, to pull at his trousers, or insist on showing him some twig or soft toy, Harvey would smile his paternal smile, and move behind Andrea, holding her by the waist, impatient to be alone with the object of his desire, begging her understanding. It worked, of course, and Andrea would fob the boy off with some excuse or other and disappear into her rooms with her impulsive lover.

Pet also observed, a little despairingly, how the rest of the staff, Ambrose included, were all gradually falling under Harvey's smooth talking spell. Because Harvey was a charmer, a real charmer, a born charmer. He knew exactly what to say to whom, in what tone, with what facial expression, and with what subtle yet detectable body language to match. It was as if he had taken a master's degree in Social Grace, and had learnt how to make people believe that the mask faithfully represented the man. So he joked with Brendan, and helped him dispose of the grass cuttings and pruned branches, putting his back into the work as a real man does, uncomplainingly, without expecting either thanks or recompense. Mr. Stein he treated with huge respect, acknowledging the man's worth, his history, his wisdom, and above all, his rank. He pretended to be speechless when confronted with Luz's superior efficiency, he had no words to express his admiration for her diligence and professionalism. Ambrose was easy. He knew that he demanded nothing more than the odd greeting, the occasional 'well done'. It had not taken him more than a second to calibrate Ambrose's mental agility, so he knew there would never be any question of rivalry or competition. Ambrose was a push over, a marginal character who posed no problem.

He thought much the same of Petunia, too, never going beyond a polite 'good day' and the praise of a specific meal. She was, he concluded almost instantly, her brother's sister. Overweight, with terrible teeth, an odour of stale cigarettes and cheap cologne about her, she was jolly enough though not particularly articulate, and as thick as a brick. A secondary member of the household staff. He politely ignored her or avoided her as much as he could.

Still, he knew he needed them on his side for the time being, so he played his part as he had learnt to do throughout his life. That does not mean that it was all deviously mapped out by Harvey in advance. There was no master plan to follow; it all came naturally, instinctively. He aspired to what every human aspires: more. He felt that he had been born superior, that he was the one-eyed man in the world of the blind, and it was his destiny, his duty almost, to accept that and act accordingly. Life had anointed him with an excellent standard of living, a healthy body, a fine education, and a sharp mind. He had no say in the matter, there could be no question of blame, we cannot be held guilty for being born, it was merely a matter of circumstance. So he automatically appraised the situation and worked out what would be the best path to follow with natural ease, always remembering that the ultimate goal was personal benefit. This was survival of the fastest. He had been gifted with the tools necessary to triumph, and he would do so, because it was his responsibility to do so. Not everyone in life can be a winner, not everyone has what it takes to succeed. But Harvey Paulson was convinced that he had been chosen at birth to stand out amongst men, to rise above the average mass of humanity, not only to survive, but to thrive. So controlling the situation, foreseeing events, responding tactfully and tactically he saw as second nature, as part of his innate ability to manipulate his world and his fellow men. There was no morality involved, no desire to do evil, only a life to be lead using the tools at hand. That he had been blessed with the finest instruments available was nothing more than chance. He would not let the opportunity escape him.

Nonetheless he was aware that the road to fortune was a rocky one, and that he had to step very carefully. The timing was not perfect. Andrea had been a widow for just three years. Internally she was still a tangle of emotions, part of her wanting to start afresh, to pick up her young life and begin to live again, whilst another side of her still wept for her loss. She could not help but see Sydney in her young son; he was like a miniature version of his dead father, a constant reminder. That on top of Alice Haute's passing away so recently, the appointing of the administrators, the legal ins and outs that she had no interest in but that had to be attended, all of this and more meant that Harvey's appearance had been more than a little rushed. But he had to grasp at this opportunity with both hands or Andrea would eventually be snapped up by someone else. That would not happen. This was a unique opportunity and he could not let it pass. He would find the patience necessary, push only as far as could be expected, demand only what she was capable of giving. He would wear her down, work his way into her life, waiting for the moment to pounce with an offer of marriage. At the right time, at the right place. In the meantime, caution and best behaviour.

Eighteen months later, just after Sydney Jr.'s fourth birthday, Andrea and Harvey were married in a side room of the local Town Hall. At Andrea's insistence it was a simple affair, more like signing the deeds of a house than a marriage ceremony. They repeated the words a little embarrassedly like children, afraid they would make a silly mistake and be laughed at. They vowed what they were expected to vow, they exchanged rings, they kissed. Twenty minutes and it was all over. There was to be no banquet, no band, no honeymoon. Andrea had begged Harvey to understand her, and he had been happy to comply. He was not interested in the paraphernalia of a wedding, the guest list, the bouquets, the awkwardness of wedding presents. He just wanted the papers signed and safely in his pocket. In a way he was grateful to Sydney for having previously supplied Andrea with a fairy tale wedding day, it had saved him the time and effort, as well as the expense.

For Andrea had become Mrs. Haute in the most traditional way imaginable. The service had taken place within the grounds of Haute House, under a white canvas marquee, with beautifully laid tables, and chairs with little dresses on them to hide their ugly legs. Catering care of the Carlton Hotel chain. The forecourt was a makeshift parking lot full of glamorous vehicles that glittered like dark gems. The pool had been filled with multi-coloured balloons that popped every so often under the early summer sun. Guests in absurd gowns and uncomfortable suits walked about like extras in a film, unsure exactly what the director expected of them. There was a protocol that only a chosen few had seen, so a stately chaos reigned, which grew in intensity with the heat of the day and the amount of alcohol imbued. After the mock solemnity of the ceremony itself, a deadly serious affair that only Mrs. Alice Haute and the sickly looking vicar seemed to appreciate, there had been speeches and dances and drunks to attend to. A one man band played incessantly, filling the air with the musical equivalent of pestering wasps. The musician/D.J. was a short man nearing his fifties, with dyed hair swept back over his shiny, suntanned skin, and an unshakeable belief that any combination of notes and rhythms was a gift of the gods: they sent him into a frenzy every time. He played his organ, he swayed his hips, he held out his arms outstretched to the indifferent crowd as if saying – I give you music!

Eventually the sun had gone down and the cavalcade had disappeared through the metal gates. The caterers went about their business, the D.J. loaded his kit into his van, family and friends retired exhausted. Andrea and Sydney were now married. Till death do us part.

That day had gone down officially as the happiest day of her life. She could not possible go through it all again.

In the weeks that followed the brief marriage ceremony, Harvey moved in. And it seemed that with each van load of his belongings that arrived he was also reassembling his original personality. The pleasantries became few and far between, shorter and sharper, pinched into caricatures of courtesy. He became brusque and off-hand, and his temper began to make an appearance. It was clear from the outset that he was going to have difficulties handling the staff, the very same staff he had so recently wooed and charmed. He had no tact, no patience, no time for fools. Things were to be done properly at the first attempt, anything less was incompetence. Instructions were to be understood straight off, because they were clear and unequivocal. In his opinion Haute House should run as smoothly as his office, and the employees should be professionals, that was why they had been hired in the first place. He had no truck with the subtleties of command, couldn't care less how the underlings felt, if they took things personally or not, if they responded to certain strategies or others. There was work to be done, and there were plenty more people out there willing to do just as a good a job under the same conditions.

He was to be called Mr. Paulson, or, as an alternative, Sir. He had wanted to suggest forms of address for Andrea, too, but soon realised that would be going too far. There was a bond between his wife and the members of the household that he could not now undo, a bond strengthened over the last few years by the unifying force of mutual loss. They would continue to call her Andrea as they had always done, just as they had called her late husband simply Sydney. The boy had now inherited that name, the suffix 'junior' having lost its usefulness. But Harvey would be respected, much as he imagined the late Mrs. Haute had been respected, as undoubtedly had her husband and all the other former owners of the estate. Mr. Paulson, if you please. Sir, for short.

Joe Stein, as acknowledged head of staff, bore the brunt of this change in attitude. In many ways he understood Harvey's complaints, even shared with him certain suggestions for improvement. It was true that the house ticked over at a slow pace, with a relaxed rhythm that could at times be infuriating. It was also true that sometimes chores were left undone, that messages were not given to the right person at the right time, that mistakes were made. Mr. Stein recognised the facts, was the first to agree. However...

That was when Harvey cut him short. No howevers, no buts, no mitigating circumstances. Efficiency. Attention to detail. Concentration. Responsibility.

Yes sir.

What Mr. Stein knew but Harvey Paulson did not, is that not everybody responds to the same therapy. For some people a simple command, clearly given with no possibility of misinterpretation, was the perfect tool with which to work. Mission accomplished. To others such an order raised a whole host of related questions, posed a full range of possible knock on effects. Luz would definitely prefer to be able to clarify the consequences of the command by asking for further information. To her it was not enough to say 'clean the windows'. She would need to know if that meant inside and out, if the curtains should be removed, if there was a certain room that should be cleaned first, if the window cleaner, read Ambrose, should drop all other chores and concentrate solely on cleaning windows, or if it should be done piecemeal. And of course there were those, Brendan for example, who did not like to be told what to do. That did not imply laziness or slovenliness. Far from it: Brendan, like his son after him, was an excellent gardener and dedicated professional. But he had to feel that the initiative came from him, had been his sovereign decision. He expected his age and his wisdom to be respected. The gardens were his domain, and nobody knew better than he did what needed doing and when. So for Brendan it was better to mention that the lawns seemed to have suffered a little from the recent weather. Ten minutes later he would be working on the grass. The chestnut trees have really grown. They would be pruned to perfection before the day was through.

Joe Stein knew these things, and a lot more. He also knew he would have to agree with Mr. Paulson on everything, show no signs of dissent, and pass the word on to the rest of them if they were to keep their jobs. All this without causing a fuss or stirring up ill-feeling. They would all have to make an effort if Harvey was to be accommodated.

The upkeep of a large house in extensive grounds is a constant battle against time, weather and nature. At the first signs of neglect window frames begin to swell and buckle, stonework crumbles, ironwork dissolves into rust. Wild plants lurk on the edges of lawns and carefully tended arbours, patiently waiting for a chance to return, to reclaim the land from which they have been evicted. The maintenance of this tiny portion of civilisation against the onslaughts of the elements was a continuous struggle, and all available able bodied men and women would need to be recruited to combat those forces. It was a matter of patience and constancy, and was the way things had been run for years. Only now there was a new boss, with a new vision, who believed that if he applied his organisational skills to the estate, then the war would not only be won, it would be the war to end all wars. At least that was the impression he wanted to create.

'Señora Luz.'

The 'señora' he used to maintain his distance.

'Yes sir?'

She was professionally unruffled, on the surface.

'I asked you for the inventory to be done at the end of every month. Have you done so?'

'I hope to have it finished by mid next week sir.'

'I need it by Monday.'

That was a challenge. He was deliberately pushing her to see how far she would go, how far she would bend, before snapping. As she had already explained, the inventory was done on a three-monthly basis, with a flexible time table, as it always had been. There had never been even the slightest incident. That irritated him. She seemed to be saying that if it was good enough for the late Alice Haute and all those that had come before her, it was certainly good enough for the likes of Harvey Paulson. Well, he was well aware of what had been the case in the past. That was not the case now. By Monday, if you please. Yes sir.

When Mr. Stein had tried to intervene he had fared no better. He had pointed out that the inventory was a very time consuming affair, and that if Señora Luz were to be asked to complete such a task once a month, it could only take away from her other duties such as cleaning. Harvey listened attentively then suggested, to a stunned Stein, that Luz spend less time gazing out of the window, less time telephoning her relatives, and more time doing her allotted chores. Or, better still, perhaps Stein himself should do the inventory? By Monday. Yes sir.

No idle hands. Harvey was a great believer in work for work's sake. To his mind it was better to mop the floors once more, even if it was totally unnecessary, than to stand around gossiping. So little by little he increased their workload with mindless chores and inventions. Brendan was to justify everything he did in the gardens. As he did not live on the premises but came in on a part-time basis, he would now be required to make a note of every bush clipped, every lawn mown, every sack of dry leaves collected and disposed of. Harvey drew up a spread sheet which was to be completed at the end of each day's work. Trees, hedges, and bushes were subdivided into three different categories: large, medium and small, with, incredibly, their relative size-time ratios already calculated. Trees and bushes in height, hedges in length. Lawns were to be estimated by the square metre, as were the flower beds. Brendan was to be allowed twenty minutes per spread sheet, and it was to be handed in to Stein at the end of each session. Harvey would then reclaim these and supposedly study them, checking to make sure Brendan was indeed as trustworthy and efficient as he was made out to be. He rarely did, that had not been the purpose. The idea was simply to make the workers know that they were being watched so that there would be no slacking, no cheating, no idleness. And that the new boss was called Harvey Paulson.

Brendan naturally hit the roof. Who does he think he is? Who does he think he's dealing with? I'm going to tell him where he can stick his spreadsheets. But when he eventually confronted Harvey, he noticed that look in his eye, the look that said 'go on, tell me where to stick my spreadsheets, go on, and I'll tell you where to stick your job'. So instead he climbed down, gruffly, showing his distaste, but ready to accept the new rules if that was what the master preferred.

We are creatures of habit, and change is not something we welcome. A memorised routine is comfortable and enables us to switch over to automatic pilot, thereby liberating the mind from the boredom of actually having to think about the task in hand. Still we accept that change happens, is a part of life's evolution, is inevitable. Adapting to the new master would be difficult, or as Joe Stein put it, challenging. But adapt they would. If they all pulled together, if they avoided silly mistakes, avoided confrontation with Mr. Paulson, if they hung close to Andrea and Sydney, then the storm would pass. Eventually the new ways would solidify into routine, and become as dearly loved and defended as their previous version.

During the week the place ticked over much as it always had, as Harvey was gone nearly all day, only returning late in the evening. Breakfast and supper was all he required, and as he was a man of fixed customs, his needs were easily attended to. Saturday was usually tolerable too, as it was used for sport, or travel, or visiting friends. But Sundays, long weekends, or seasonal holidays became increasingly indigestible.

Then he would stroll around the house and the grounds like an overseer, like an insufferable, overcritical supervisor doing his rounds. At first he had made the mistake of allowing Andrea to accompany him on these tours, but he had soon realised that she was far too soft for managerial responsibilities. She treated the staff almost as if they were a group of volunteers that should be thanked for their efforts despite the mediocre results. Encouragement rather than punishment. She greeted them all with a smile and a genuine concern for their well-being, and appeared to accept any feeble excuse as a matter of course, as if further inquiry would be considered rude, or a lack of faith in their capabilities. So before setting off on his tour of the grounds Harvey would shake her off with some excuse or other and take on the windmills on his own.

His favourite target was Ambrose, because Ambrose Ork was an easy prey. When Harvey had cornered Joe Stein, and started to pile up the work on him, there had been a tacit negotiation taking place. Harvey would push as far as he could, Stein would resist as far as he could. If either one of them overstepped the mark, then Joe Stein would be forced to leave, which was in neither party's interest. Joe Stein was a necessary part of Haute House, and substituting him would be both difficult and impractical. The same applied to Señora Luz, who was virtually irreplaceable. Luckily she knew that, and in silence, but with elegant firmness, drew her lines. Mr. Paulson respected these limits, because he believed that everybody should mark their territory, should state clearly and honestly what they are prepared to accept, and what is simply nonnegotiable. Brendan too had made it clear that Haute House was not the only large house in the district willing to hire his by now legendry skills. So the inventory fell back little by little to its original three monthly routine, Brendan filled out his forms from memory in under five minutes, Stein collected them and handed them over to Harvey, who threw them in the bin. Petunia Ork managed to keep a low profile, and successfully avoided the new master by sticking to the kitchens and the nursery. She knew when he was approaching, and so slipped off. On the odd occasion that he sought her out and made it clear who was the new boss, she simply nodded and agreed to everything he suggested or demanded. Later she went about as always, heedless of his words. If that's what he wants to hear, she told her brother. Just steer clear of him and avoid head on clashes, he just wants to be the king of the castle, that's all, he's no more than a bloody big kid. Just say yes, ok?

Ambrose followed her advice to the letter. He let Harvey walk all over him without the slightest trace of self defence or rebellion. He would carry out his new master's instructions to the best of his abilities, then patiently wait around while Harvey told him how badly he had done this or that, what a fool he was, how he had better watch his step and do better in the future. Or else. As Ambrose didn't put up even a token resistance, Mr. Paulson could not help but be cruel. Here was a man who would obey his every command and take any abuse without so much as a murmur of complaint. In short, an idiot. And idiots get what they deserve.

In Ambrose's presence Harvey became malicious and psychologically sadistic. He had the illogical sensation that Ambrose deliberately chose to be slow off the mark just to annoy people like Harvey. His weakness was infuriating, and the further Ambrose withdrew, the further Harvey advanced, hunting him down, persecuting him. The more Ambrose ceded, the more Harvey demanded of him, as if his superiority grew proportionately to Ambrose's inferiority. Mr. Paulson was the cutting edge of evolution, a creature designed for competence and success. Mr. Ork was a throwback, a failed specimen, and therefore totally superfluous to any notion of progress. So he would send him on mindless errands, setting him tasks that were absurd and designed only to ridicule, to underline Ambrose's lack of criteria, his pitiful submission. He would wait until Ambrose had finished for the day before ordering him to clean out the rubbish bins. He would catch him just about to leave the premises on his day off, and make him clean up all the dog shit he could find in the grounds, supplying him with a stick and a plastic bag. One day he made him strip the storeroom of its contents and fittings, only to change his mind and say that he now wanted everything back to its original form. He appeared to be intent on driving Ambrose to his limit, to the breaking point where the man would eventually have to say no, enough is enough, I can go no further.

It was the very same Harvey who was so respectful towards his parents and peers, so socially adept and correct, who now took secret pleasure in torturing Ambrose, in making him writhe. He was like a domineering father, who beats his wife and terrorises his children because he can, but who stands in awe of a uniform, a rule book, the scent of wealth. And Ambrose was like that man's wife or child, unable to resist, unsure even if it was his place to resist. Mr. Paulson was the boss. Joe Stein and Pet had warned him to avoid confrontation. So he just got on with whatever he had to do, limiting himself to private complaints, or out of earshot grumbles, and the consolation of being able to rant to his heart's content to his sister and the rest of the staff.

It was something they all took part in, a purging they all enjoyed. Their insults and interjections were interchangeable, only varying in the amount of swear words employed. The overwhelming verdict was that Harvey had tricked his way into Andrea's heart and into their world, leading them to believe he was 'nice enough' when really he was a scheming, megalomaniacal bastard.

'Thinks he's the fucking Lord of the Manor!'

'I *hate* the way he follows me about.'

'What I can't understand is how she doesn't notice what he's really like. How can she be so *blind*?'

'She does, she does, but it's too late now, isn't it?'

'Maybe there's another side to her that we don't know.'

'He gives me the fucking creeps. There's something in his eye...'

'Poor kid, that's what I say. Poor little kid.'

'And he's got it in for Bro.'

'He's got it in for the lot of us.'

'Why oh why did she have to go and marry a bastard like that?'

'Give me Sydney any day, *he* was a gentleman.'

'She'd turn in her grave.'

'He'll be the end of us. '

'Fucking bastard.'

It was then very hard for Pet not to say 'I told you so'. But even if she had they would probably have forgotten her words by now and swear that she had never warned them at all. So she just joined in with the general abuse.

Andrea watched as Harvey strutted about the place on his day off. His attitude amused her. He was so incapable of separating work from leisure, tried so hard to run the place as if it were a busy city office, would spend ages following the staff around to make sure they completed their allotted tasks well and on time. But it was like driving into a brick wall. Nothing he said or did seemed to make the slightest difference, and she assumed that one day he would realise that and relax a little. In the meantime she was grateful for his interest in the running of the place; it was a weight off her mind.

Anyway it was nothing compared to her real concern. Harvey and little Sydney did not appear to hit it off. At first that had been natural enough; they were strangers. Still she had hoped that over the months a bond would grow between them, something approaching a father and son relationship, albeit it in a watered down fashion. But so far neither of them had made any progress whatsoever. The little boy, understanding in his own way that he was not welcome in Harvey's presence, simply acted as if his step-father did not exist. Which the astute Harvey then used to his favour, claiming that the child totally ignored him. That Harvey was responsible for the stand-off was blatantly apparent, but he took refuge in his man's world, in his professional career, in his lack of experience in child rearing. He begged Andrea for comprehension, and received it. These things can't be forced. Time would put everything in its place, he argued, so more time, please. There was little she could do, so she acceded. As long as he promised to make an effort, when he could, if he could. Anything would do. A small toy every so often, a walk in the grounds, maybe read a book together. Or watch T.V. Harvey would see what he could do. They left it at that.

In reality Harvey *was* making an effort. He was striving to come across as the willing but inept step-father when the truth was that he could not bear the child. Not at all. In fact he was beginning to hate him. As far as he could see the boy had no saving graces. He was the very image of his dead father, blonde and beautiful, bright and cheerful. Maybe if he had not resembled the late Sydney Haute so much Harvey could have forgiven him his lineage and taken him a little more to heart. As it was he saw the child as a rival, a constant reminder of things past, a permanent source of jealousy. Because Andrea was not a divorcee, she was a widow. Under normal circumstances she would still have been married to the man she loved, and would have formed a perfectly happy family, with Sydney Jr. as its centrepiece. Her truncated love for her deceased husband now found an unnatural outlet in her son. She adored him. Which meant that the poor boy was pampered and spoilt. Which meant that he was becoming capricious and wilful. Which made Harvey hate him all the more. The kid threw tantrums, respected no-one and nothing, screamed until he had his way. In fact he was starting to become the unbearable child Harvey himself had once been. Little by little Sydney Haute was being turned into a mini dictator. And they expected Harvey to read to him, to hug him, to kiss him goodnight!

As if that was not enough, the whole estate had been left to this obnoxious child, to be inherited on his coming of age. Andrea had been well catered for, it was true, but the real wealth had been placed in the hands of outsiders for the next fourteen years or so. Harvey had acquired certain rights and privileges by marrying Andrea, but the fact remained that Sydney Jr. was the real master of the House. The stone in Harvey's shoe. But as all this was unmentionable, Harvey kept it to his chest, preferring simply to be absent as much as possible like so many busy professional parents. Let Andrea and that fat Petunia woman take care of the boy, he had better things to do.

Like hounding Ambrose.

Harvey was fascinated by Ambrose. For an intelligent person it is not easy to understand why others learn so slowly, find it so hard to retain basic information. New facts were burnt into Harvey's brain cells with a branding iron. With Ambrose it was like trying to scratch your name on a bathroom tile, an exercise in stubborn repetition. Eventually, after a thousand attempts, he would grasp the concept, as his father had shown by drilling into him the skills required in electrical wiring, but it was a painfully slow process. Over the years Ambrose had learnt how to carry out a great number of useful jobs, but each time he needed to be taught with patience, his efforts encouraged, his mistakes forgiven and duly corrected. Harvey had no time for that, and lost his temper at the first signs of ineptitude. He told him to strip the paint off the boiler house door, 'use the blow torch if necessary'. Ambrose burnt not only the doorframe but also his overalls. Harvey docked it out of his wages. Changing sash cords is a job for professionals, but Ambrose was being paid to maintain the premises, so he would just have to learn how to do it. At his first attempt he was bawled out by a furious Harvey. The cost of the reparation was again taken from his monthly salary.

'What *can* you do, Ambrose? Apart from annoy me?'

He had wanted to say basic electrics, plumbing, painting, fixing roof tiles and guttering, most builders work and so on, but wisely chose not to reply.

Incredibly to Harvey, it seemed that this learning deficit, this apparent lack of a working memory, also meant that Ambrose rarely bore a grudge. Despite the abuse and the foul manners Harvey displayed whilst in his presence, Ambrose invariably met his boss with a cheery 'good morning, sir'. Not once had he complained to Harvey's face, not once had he refused to see through even the most menial task, not once had he tried to make himself invisible at weekends as Harvey knew the others did. Was it that Ambrose had a faulty memory? Was that why he could not learn things properly? Was that the reason why he still behaved towards Harvey with deep respect, as if Harvey were his amiable benefactor? Questions that Harvey was unable to answer.

Looking back it is difficult to tell exactly when Harvey realised that Ambrose could be used to his advantage. Given the available information it is impossible to deduce whether Harvey's actions were based on instinct or cunning, if the decisions he took were made subconsciously or if they were part of a carefully calculated plan. In hindsight it is a debate between those who claim that what happened is due to the nature of the beast, and those who prefer the conspiracy theory. Either way most would agree that the letter to Ambrose from Harvey's lawyer was a pivotal point in the tragedy.

Ambrose didn't receive mail, so it was a huge surprise to everybody when the postman explained that there was a certified letter for Ambrose Ork, and that he would have to sign for it. Joe Stein found him in the back yard sorting out the new recycling bins.

'A letter for you, Bro, a certified letter. You have to go and sign for it. At the front. '

Ambrose looked at him quizzically.

'Well go on, he's waiting for you.'

'For me?'

'No, for the king of Persia. Put that down and go and get the letter. It's for you.'

Ambrose felt special then, as if it were his birthday or something. A letter, a certified letter, for him! Who could it be, what could it be? It had to be something special or it would not arrive by certified post. He scurried off as fast as he could so as not to keep the postman waiting.

As soon as the deliverer had left, and in the presence of Joe Stein and sister Pet, he carefully opened the letter, which did not look as if it contained a pleasant surprise. It was from a firm of lawyers in the city, addressed to Mr. Ambrose Ork, and written on very serious and pompous headed paper. Pet and Stein shared nervous glances. Ambrose read it, but he was not really reading it at all. He did not understand most of the language used, or at least not in that way. It was long-winded and deliberately clumsy, as if they were playing a game, hiding the real meaning of the message from him for some strange reason. It certainly did not appear to be friendly, anyway. He handed it to Pet, who had a similar reaction. Mumbo jumbo it sounded to her, though very much in the line of the eviction papers they had been served way back when. It was not to be trusted, so she handed it over to Joe Stein, who knew all about such things. Mr. Stein read it through slowly, more than once. Then he asked both of them to follow him to his office.

There they sat again, once more back in Stein's office, though this time they were not sweating due to the heat. Mr. Stein shook his head, and when he spoke it was almost in a whisper.

'This,'

he flicked at the embossed sheet of paper with his fingernails as if it were something despicable,

'is an official warning, sent to you, Bro, from the boss, Mr. H. Paulson, via these lawyers, acting on his behalf so to speak.

Basically it is a complaint. They, he, complains about your work, the quality of your work, your capabilities and so on. It lists a number of incidents... the window repair job......the doorframe...... some wiring in the store room.......with details of costs. It states that you are taking on jobs for which you are not qualified, with special reference to..... just a minute....... hmm electrical installations....and..... blah, blah......You'll have to watch your step from now on, Bro, he's got it in for you all right.'

Pet held Stein's gaze.

'Did you know anything about this? '

It was an accusation that Mr. Stein did not take very well.

'Of course not! This has taken me by surprise just as much as it has all of us. It is not the procedure, not the way to do things. Not at all. And yes, he should have spoken to me first, I should have been informed. This is not the way. Believe me, I had no idea.'

Pet was convinced, and wanted to apologise for having doubted Stein.

'What a... bar steward! Get the lawyers to write a letter instead of doing it himself. I thought he was supposed to be a fucking lawyer himself, jumped up little....shit. What else does it say? Is he going to sack him?'

'No, no. At least not yet. It's not as easy as that, but this is a first step. He's on to you, Bro, so best be on your best behaviour. This is an official warning, I don't suppose it'll stop there.'

'What do you mean?'

Mr. Stein frowned over his rimless glasses.

'I mean he won't stop there. You can't give him any more cause. He wants you out.'

'I don't give him no cause, do I?'

Ambrose pleaded. His sister nodded.

'If he goes, I go.'

Defiant, loyal Pet.

'And maybe that's what he wants, too. Who knows what he wants, he certainly doesn't consult me. Maybe that's exactly what he wants, to get rid of us all.'

She hadn't thought of that. Neither had Joe Stein until that moment.

'Sneaky little.... What do we do, answer it? Do we need a lawyer? We had a lawyer once, not that it did much good...'

Joe held up his palms as if to say 'calm, calm'.

'No. It has been delivered, Bro has signed. Leave it at that. If we start contesting every point it'll only make things worse. Let sleeping dogs lie and all that. Act as if nothing has happened, o.k.? I'm sorry, Bro.'

Ambrose thanked him for that. Then he left with his sister so that she could explain to him in layman's terms what on earth was going on.

Strangely enough it was Harvey who acted as if nothing had happened. He never mentioned the letter; not to Ambrose, not to Stein, and by all accounts not even to Andrea. He had made his point, it seemed. Ambrose had been called to order, job done. Stein kept the original, Pet stored a photocopy in an envelope in her knicker drawer, where she assumed no-one would ever look, and everyone did their best not to remember the incident, as if by naming it again it would suddenly leap back to life.

Even stranger was that from that moment on Harvey treated Ambrose more kindly. He abruptly stopped ambushing him during his off duty hours, the ridiculous jobs were dropped, and even Ambrose's errors were tolerated to a certain degree. The official warning had been like a punch in the face from the tough but fair sheriff. Ambrose was supposed to take it like a man and get on with it. The status quo had been established, there was no need for more. At least that's how they saw it at the time; it was the only interpretation that made sense.

As if the letter incident wasn't enough to confuse all concerned, it was round about that time that Harvey started to show a timid interest in little Sydney. At first they were small gestures, almost imperceptible to outsiders, but very welcome to Andrea and Sydney himself. A little more patience when listening to the boy's stories, a brief holding of hands while they waited for Andrea to finish getting ready, the occasional 'my', as in 'how's my boy this morning?' Perhaps the ice was beginning to melt? Perhaps Harvey would learn to accept and even love the boy after all. There was hope, thought Andrea. And it was the memory of that possibility, the chance of a true relationship developing, that she clung to through it all, like a lifeline. She would never be able to believe the cynics, because that would be too much, that would be unbearable.

Harvey's change of mood meant that for a long year the atmosphere at Haute House returned to something very much like it had been before his arrival. The settled routine allowed them all to relax, to loosen up and live a little. The place ticked over with professional ease, with hardly an incident worthy of note. The family, because now it could be called a family, appeared to be united and growing in strength day by day. Andrea was still infatuated by her new man, who in his turn had not for a second unattended her. He still sent flowers every so often, perfectly out of the blue, and she never knew when she would wake up to find a perfume or a trinket by her pillow. But what really made her feel happy was that he had taken to going for a stroll through the grounds with Sydney at weekends, if the weather allowed, and every so often sat with him through some cartoon fantasy, pretending to be fascinated by the infantile plot. She knew how much effort on his part this required, and she was very grateful to him for attempting to bond with the boy. Because Sydney was, as the saying goes, difficult. She realised now that she had spoilt him, and that what he now needed was not only love and affection, but a clear routine, a touch of discipline. Above all the child needed to learn to respect his elders, to learn some manners, to understand his place in the order of things. It was a task she did not feel able to see through on her own, as she knew she would capitulate at the first tear. Anyway, educating a son requires coherence, and Andrea was not the most stable of mothers. She would chide him for his behaviour one day, and laugh at it the next. She would put up with tantrums, but sharply snap at him over the most trifling affair. She would set up ultimatums, but let them pass without a fight. Sydney did his best under such circumstances, which meant looking after number one and getting away with as much as possible without suffering too much. By the time he was five he was considered by all to be a spoilt brat.

Andrea had hoped that Pet could help her out, and Sydney was often to be found in the kitchen or the laundry room with her. But Pet was not a mother, she was a hired hand. So she looked after the boy, but she did not feel it was her duty or her position to educate the lad. As long as he behaved himself in her presence, as long as he stayed out of trouble so she could hand him back safe and sound, that was enough. It was not her job to teach the child manners, that was Andrea's task.

'He needs a brother. Or a sister,'

Pet pronounced one day to Andrea. She made sure that it sounded jolly and jokey, even a little risqué, but she said it with a purpose. The comment was not lost on Andrea. It was a possibility that had crossed her mind more than once, to the point that she had even mentioned it, again casually, carefully, to Harvey. He had not been amused.

'Do you really think the time, the timing, is right? That it's the right time?'

Seeing the disappointment on her face he continued.

'I mean, it's not that I think it's a bad idea, no, of course not. It would be fantastic! But not yet, not so soon, not with little Sydney being such a .. handful.'

Once more he asked for patience, once more it was granted. As he always said, first things first.

Still, she thought that his influence would help straighten out young Sydney. Harvey was always in control, very constant, very correct. He had perfect manners when required, knew how to behave in every situation, understood that an education is vital. And having been a little brat himself, he knew all Sydney's tricks and tactics, and could outwit him every time. So to notice that for the first time Harvey was taking an interest in Sydney filled her with immense joy. Perhaps when he saw that the boy was less of a handful, then... Everything would work out, she was sure. For now, enjoy the present.

It was a period of peace and tranquillity. In the cyclical nature of things, the lull before the storm.

4

The day Ambrose left prison he was led to an open plan office in the administrative building where he was made to sign for his meager belongings. One electric shaver, Phillips, one mobile phone, Nokia, one radio, Puretone, with earpiece.... He could have sworn that there had been a watch, too, but maybe Pet had taken it with her. Anyway he had a new one now, Swatch, so he said nothing. These items were handed to him on a plastic tray like those used at airports or for sterilizing scalpels in operating theatres. He picked them up and started to stuff them into his pockets. The warden, Peters, one of the most popular guards along with young Mudda, watched Ambrose wonder where to put his shaver.

'Just a second, Mr. Ork'

He rummaged around under a desk and produced a plastic shopping bag.

'Here, best use this. Didn't you think of bringing a bag?'

He watched as Ambrose clumsily transferred the objects to the shopping bag. Obviously not.

'Thanks.'

They escorted him through a number of locked doors to the main entrance. It was a new prison, with a modern design of sheet glass, open spaces and highly polished floors. Pot plants added a warmer touch. It was the joker style of the moment, and served for museums, hotel lobbies, tax offices and crematoriums alike.

He was relieved to see that nobody was waiting for him. 'Nobody' meant Pet, of course, who else was there? Unless she had nipped outside for a quick cigarette. He decided to check. The automatic doors slid open, and a blast of heat greeted him as if he had opened the door to hell. The taxi stand was empty, and apart from the shuttle bus which would take him into civilization, the place was understandably deserted. Who wants to be hanging around in that heat outside a provincial prison in the back end of nowhere? He strolled over to the mini bus, but it was empty, the doors closed. Time for a cigarette. So she had fallen for it. He felt slightly proud of himself for that. He had never been good at lying, and he'd feared that she would see through his ruse and turn up anyway. He had fooled her into thinking that his release had been delayed for some bureaucratic reason or other beyond his grasp, and she had apparently been happy to believe that.

The prison bus eventually took him into town, free of charge, and then turned him loose into the summer heat. What he was supposed to do next was not explained, or if it had been he had not understood a word of it. There had been chats by social assistants about reinsertion and reorientation and rehabilitation, words far too similar sounding for him to be able to distinguish, let alone retain. Now he was stranded, dressed in, or rather stuffed into, his best suit, swinging a plastic bag and sweating profusely. A free man. Luckily he had a plan of his own.

Which was why he had to spare Pet, had to keep her at arm's length. Although truth be told he had not seen much of her over the last few years. She had hitched up with a man called Doug, someone Ambrose had never seen, not even in a photo, and this Doug character had hauled her off to Wollbury where she was now working as a waitress. That made it increasingly more difficult to visit, what with the distance and the unearthly hours of the bar. At least that was how she had excused herself back then. Was it true, or was Doug to blame? He imagined him sometimes as a burly pimp, balding, greasy and pot-bellied, bossing his sister about and snatching up her wages to blow on whatever vices were in fashion. But no, she had looked apologetic and sincere, and always spoke well of Doug. He had to trust Pet; she was all he had left. So they limited themselves to phone calls, once a week in theory, more like once a month in practice, and the odd letter. He had preferred to lie to her on paper, as he was sure she would have noticed something in his voice had he attempted it over the phone. Now she thought he wasn't due out for another month. More than enough time.

He had been given a list of addresses and telephone numbers of various social services departments, as well as a number of websites to consult, but to all effects he was now homeless, destitute. He had enough money to last for about three months if he behaved normally, more if he was very careful. This was money he had earned diligently whilst inside, and which had been set aside for him for the day of his release. He had expected to receive it in an envelope, almost like a wedding present, but instead he had been handed a savings book in his name. Sign here. Thankfully it did not make any mention to the government institution from which he had recently emerged. The savings book he tucked into his inside jacket pocket. The rest of his information sheets he dumped into the first litter bin he came across, along with his copy of all the documents he had been forced to sign without knowing what they were about. He wouldn't need them now.

Ambrose had another address that was much more important. Or rather he had directions and instructions of how to make contact, committed to memory, which was safer. Spotty had been very specific on that point – nothing written down. It had to be pure memory, like spies, that way they could not hang any charges on you should anything go wrong. Spotty was a stickler for detail. Ambrose was also convinced that this was the only way to proceed. Whatever happened he could not incriminate Spotty, not after all his help and encouragement. So he memorized it all over and over again until he could recite it in his sleep. There could be no hiccups; that was vital.

So working from memory he began the hunt for his old cell mate, who, he hoped, had not forgotten their plan, or that today was the seventeenth. The route began at St. Mary's, his back to the main doors, so he trekked off in that direction. It was quite a way, especially under that sun, but he preferred to walk, to enjoy the sensation of space and the lack of any real timetable to work to. Anyway, although it was deadly serious, this was also fun, this was adventure. He picked out the landmarks as if they formed part of a pirates' treasure map. Turn left at the church, take the second on the right, there is a letter box on the corner. Go past the factory gates and on to the embankment. He clung to the shadows as much as he could to avoid the punishing heat of late afternoon, but also because it seemed right; it was what a spy would do. Surreptitious, as spotty would say. He thought that wearing an out of season suit and carrying a shopping bag might even help. Who had ever seen a spy dressed like that? Eventually he realised he had reached his destination, the place marked with an x in his mind.

It was a rundown bar called the Bandstand, though why it had been baptized with such a name was difficult to discern, it was just another door and another shop-like window sandwiched between equally disheveled establishments. The main entrance was propped open, and inside it was as dark as a cavern, especially after the bright light of the intense summer sun. Perhaps that was a trick, so that those lurking inside could gain an advantage over the newly-arrived who would blink and stare blindly into the hidden recesses of the joint trying to make out if there was anybody there or not. Ambrose checked his mental map once more, then took the plunge.

It took some time for him to get used to the dimly lit interior of the bar, but little by little he started to make out shadowy figures impaled on stools along the bar at regular intervals as if placed there on purpose by an invisible hostess. A slovenly barman, not fat, but slack, droopy, as if he were melting slowly, watched him with expressionless eyes, a look he had cultivated over the years because it was the best way to survive. 'You looking at me?' 'I don't look at nothing no more.' The customers turned to Ambrose, weighed him up in a matter of seconds, and recoiled back into their allotted spaces. In the back room, he had said, in one of the booths. Ambrose slipped by without raising suspicion, without aggravating anyone, as he had learnt to do in prison. It was body language. You are just doing your own thing, minding your own business, and you are not embarrassed by that, don't need to apologise or ask permission. No threat to anyone, either. Just going on through to the back, nothing else.

And there he was, just as he had promised, sat in the corner under a mirror which was an advertisement for a long forgotten beer, clad in a skin tight white v-neck T-shirt, a huge gold chain dangling down almost to his stomach. His shaven head, his goatee beard, a glass of beer set before him like a relic. Good old Spotty, a man to trust. Ambrose sat down opposite him, held out his hand, and smiled.

'Hi Spotty, it's me, Bro. I didn't know if you'd remember. Today is the seventeenth. But I knew you wouldn't forget.'

Spotty had forgotten, completely, but that didn't matter much because he was where he said he would be. After six o'clock he was always there, and would only leave when he ran out of money or credit or the capacity to stand on his own two feet without help.

Spotty half stood up.

'Bro! Today is your big day, and I forget?'

He shook his hand violently.

'The seventeenth, eh? Now, what was supposed to happen on the seventeenth? My Mum's birthday? Hey Stan, get a beer for my old friend Ambrose.'

'No, no, thanks, no.'

Spotty leant over the table.

'You got no money, Bro?'

'Oh yes, I got a bit for now, but I don't want a beer.'

'OK. Make that a beer and a…..?'

'Something without alcohol.'

'And a coke. Coke ok?'

'Er, yeah, fine, a coke's fine'.

Spotty sat down and spread his legs wide open; he had made a full recovery by now.

'Nice bag.'

Ambrose laughed.

'I didn't have anywhere to put my stuff, so Peters gave me this.'

'Peters! That'll be where he keeps his knitting.'

The reference was lost on Ambrose, but he laughed anyway. You had to laugh at all the jokes, even if they were about gays or wife beating or killing cops, it was part of the code, made you one of them.

Spotty frowned, and looked down at his beer.

'So you doubted me, eh Bro? For a moment there? Didn't know if I'd keep my word, eh?'

He let that sink in. Bro said nothing, as he had learnt to do over the years.

'The seventeenth, Bro, the seventeenth. I got that burnt into my mind like an engraving, like a laser.'

He tapped the side of his head.

'So I just came in here and waited, just like I said I would.'

Another pause.

'And here I am!'

Ambrose took in the sight. Spotty was obviously still working out, you could see his muscles bulging from under his carefully chosen T-shirt, but he had lost something. The hardness, the straining, the parading, all that terseness seemed to have been hidden under a sheen of relaxation, of relative comfort, of too many beers. Spotty had been a free man for over six months now, and it showed. But his eyes remained as alert and keen as ever.

They had a few cigarettes, some more drinks, and talked about the only thing they had in common – the prison and its inhabitants. They recalled anecdotes and incidents, relived for a time their shared experience like ex soldiers do. But they both realized that it was only small talk, a common courtesy, a traditional ritual. That was not why Ambrose was there.

Spotty's face changed, grew serious.

'So you're going through with it.'

It was not a question. He had seen the serene determination on Ambrose face, his joy at having found Spotty waiting for him. The fact that he was alone on the day of his release, that no-one had come to meet him, had not been lost on Spotty. The man sitting before him looked a little ridiculous in a suit not meant for summer, too small for him now he had taken up weight lifting, albeit it without much success. Sitting there hugging a coke, waiting for instructions. He felt sorry for Ambrose, as he often did. But it was Bro's decision, not his.

'Ok. Drink up and we'll go to my place. Sure you weren't followed?'

He asked that as a kind of joke. Who on earth would want to follow someone like Ambrose? But Bro answered sincerely. He had taken precautions, he was sure he had not been tailed. Spotty shook his head imperceptibly.

'Come on, then, we'd better get things straight. Sooner the better.'

Spotty asked for the bill and waited while Ambrose settled it before leading him back out into the street. The sun had moved on a little, but the heat remained, bouncing back off the walls like a blow torch.

After so much mystery and caution, the memorized route, the stealthy approach, their secret rendezvous, after taking so much trouble not to be caught, walking down the street together in the plain light of day seemed a little foolhardy to Ambrose. Weren't they supposed to be extremely careful? What if they were seen together? Or followed? Why was Spotty so apparently nonchalant about it all? It made no sense. But Spotty was the genius; he knew what he was doing. There would no doubt be a very good explanation, something that would make it all fall into place. But Ambrose wouldn't ask, that would be putting his friend into question. No, he would trust him and do as he was told. To a point at least.

Before a metal garden gate which gave on to a wild, semi-abandoned patch of garden, Spotty told Ambrose to wait. He disappeared round the back of the tattered bungalow, which although in urgent need of repair was still clearly inhabited, with flower pots on the porch and clean curtains hanging at the windows. The front door swung open, and Spotty gestured to Bro to make it quick.

Inside it was dark, but the heat had worked its way through the thin walls and hung in the air like pending doom. Ambrose caught a glimpse of a bedroom as he walked along the corridor. It was a woman's room, he knew, far too tidy and adorned to have been Spotty's. He passed on into the dining room cum kitchen.

'This is Myra's place. She's...'

He winked at Bro.

'... a friend of a friend. Great kid. A sensitive soul.'

By which he meant that Myra, like the folk back at the Bandstand bar, knew about losing, knew how difficult it was to survive on the streets, knew that the odds were stacked against them and that the good life would never be theirs, or at least not for long. Even if they did hit lucky, they all knew it wouldn't last. It was their lot, so they had best stick together as best they could.

He told Bro to get him a beer, but in the fridge there was only a jug of water. Better than nothing. He switched on the fan that sat on the table and aimed it at them both. Now at least they could breathe. Ambrose took off his jacket and rolled up his shirt sleeves. They drank their water in silence for a while, listening to the whirr of the electric fan.

'You got to be lucky, see.'

Spotty often did that, just plunged into a conversation as if picking up from where he'd left off. He knew it confused Ambrose, and enjoyed the effect it had on him. But it was not merely a trick. It was his philosophy, his world view, and he felt he deserved to be heard. Spotty was no fool, he had been around and seen things most people wouldn't care to see and done things he was not particularly proud of. And he had learnt things from all of that. And by talking, by going over it again out loud, he got the impression that he understood parts of it, could maybe pass on the lesson to others, or at least sum it up so that he could remember the lesson himself.

He talked to the ceiling, happy to have an audience no matter who, even happier to have Ambrose there, he was a good listener, he was always willing to learn, always trying even if he never got there in the end.

'It's all a question of luck. I don't mean good luck or bad luck, just luck. What is good luck to some is bad luck to others, and there's nothing you can do about that.'

He was getting bogged down. Good and bad, treacherous ground. Time to bail out; Ambrose would be none the wiser.

'Well, maybe there is, but that's another story.'

Ambrose settled back in his chair and said nothing. It was like being back in his cell. Now Spotty would talk, on and on, building up his theories, working on them until he was happy with the outcome. There would be pauses, and self correction, and the odd rhetorical question it was not polite to try to answer. It was soothing to Ambrose; all those words so well put together, all those incredibly subtle ideas threaded together one by one until he had made a necklace of nuances and concepts. He knew it would all be too much to grasp, too intricate to fully understand, but he loved the sound of it, it was like listening to someone think.

Spotty had been thinking about luck for some time now, ever since Myra, recriminating him, had said that he was lucky to be there. Was he? Or was he unlucky to be there? Is luck a theory of relativity? Was he 'relatively' lucky or unlucky? True, he was out of jail now, enjoying her generosity, a free man. But he was also unemployed, unemployable probably, with a criminal record, struggling to get by as best he could, living off his old friendships until they wore too thin to be of any help.

'You can't change your luck for the better, Bro, but you can change it for the worse. And you can change others' for the worse, too, if you put your mind to it.'

Ambrose had heard all this about luck before, because Spotty was prone to repetition, but he did not agree with his friend on the subject. For Ambrose it was all about consequence, of sequences and movement, of dominoes and butterflies. Which meant that the course of events could be changed by direct or indirect action. Except he could never put any of that into words. Words were a hinderance to him, not a help. Over the years he had seen the look of bewilderment, surprise, even anger, on people's faces as he had tried in vain to express himself, to explain what he was thinking, or rather feeling. He faltered, he stuttered, he fell silent in shame. Stringing words together like pearls on a necklace was not for him. Spotty had informed him once that ideas and emotions can only exist if there is a word for them, that things have to be named to become real. That was nonsense. Words were invented precisely to translate ideas and feelings so that others could share them and hopefully understand them too. The problem was finding the right word, or inventing a new one if all else failed.

So all that philosophy had to remain inside, because the moment he attempted to give shape to what he intuitively suspected to be true, he would become muddled and confused, more often than not coming across as an idiot. A complete idiot, as they all liked to remind him.

But just for the record he did not agree with spotty on everything, was capable of reaching his own internal conclusions. Now he had no-one to look after him, he had learnt to fend for himself.

Yet he also understood that he could never say anything of the sort to Spotty, so he played his part, as always. Ambrose nodded, he was listening, please continue.

'How do we do that? How do we change our luck, or somebody else's luck, for the worse? Me and you know the answer to that, Bro, me and you and a load of other people we know too. It all happens when we prey on each other.'

Ambrose understood 'pray', but he wasn't really following the discourse anyway so it didn't make much difference. The speech was not aimed at Ambrose but at Humanity.

'Matti McCormack tried to prey on me, and he changed my luck for the worse. He didn't know he was going to die into the bargain, that was impossible to calculate, but it was his determination to prey on me and my family that led to my change of luck, for the worse.'

He was referring to what he termed his brush with fate.

The Dodd family, of which Richard, otherwise known as Spotty, was the eldest son, had suffered an accident. Mrs. Janet Dodd had been travelling in the back of a car driven by a male friend of hers, in the company of another couple. They had been enjoying themselves at a number of bars. On the way back home, along Park Avenue South to be precise, the car had driven straight into an oncoming coach. The occupant of the passenger seat died instantly, being thrown out of the car by the force of the impact. She had not been wearing her seat belt. The driver also died later at hospital after emergency operations failed to save his life. The occupants of the back seat of the car were both seriously injured. Mrs. Janet Dodd would never walk again.

'Luck, you see, just a question of keeping out of the way.'

As a third party occupant of the vehicle Mrs. Dodd's medical care was guaranteed. It was not until it became clear that she would require constant medical attention that her case became of great interest to the insurance company. Mr. Matti McCormack was assigned the task of finding or inventing a loophole through which the company could wash its hands of the costly Mrs. Dodd. He set about his task with dedicated professionalism.

He discovered that the driver at the time of the accident had been drinking. Could they evade responsibility on those grounds? He also discovered that Mrs. Janet Dodd was a divorcee who had left her three young children at home that night so that she could party. She had maintained relations with the drunk driver. Could a smear campaign help? He questioned all of her medical examinations and demanded that 'independent' practitioners be asked to give an 'unbiased' diagnosis and estimation of her needs.

The name McCormack soon became synonymous with evil and enemy in the Dodd household. How could this man behave in such an insidious, destructive way? It was not as if it was *his* money. He was not much to look at, average height, quite fit for his age, clipped hair graying at the temples, perfectly aligned teeth, clear blue eyes that never so much as flinched. He had an automated machine way of talking, as if the words that came from his mouth had no real meaning, no real significance, were of no consequence. He told them that his job was to inform. He informed them that it was his duty to make sure the company was not the victim of insurance fraud.

'She's in a fucking wheelchair! How do you fake that?'

To which Mr. McCormack had very slightly shrugged, almost as if to say 'we'll see'.

'Accidents, catastrophes, tragedies, they are all out there, surrounding us like flies around shit, ready to hit without warning. Could be anyone. Could be your own mother, Bro. It's like a bag of marbles failing onto the floor, you never know where they'll end up, it's crazy, chaotic, unpredictable. As unpredictable as marbles dropped on a marble floor. Marbles on marble. They bounce all around you, and if you're unlucky, one hits you and wham! It's over.'

They smoked. Spotty reflected on what he had just said, Bro sat patiently waiting for him to finish, enjoying the sound of his cell mate's voice and the hum of the fan.

His brush with fate came one morning in December. The door bell rang, and his younger brother Danny told him it was 'that fucking insurance man again'. Richard 'Spotty' Dodd opened the door.

'What do you want?'

Matti McCormack was not easily ruffled.

'Good day to you, Mr. Dodd. May I?'

He made as if to enter.

'No. Stay where the fuck you are. What do you want with us, want to suck our blood again. They cut off payments.'

'They are under review, that's not the same. Once they have been reviewed by our experts..'

'And what are we supposed to do while you bastards 'review' the payments, eh?'

Matti McCormack took the three steps that led to the front door of the Dodd house. He was not prepared to be sworn at by his client's offspring. He had come to inform her, and her alone.

'I have come to talk to your mother. If you don't mind.'

It was then that Spotty kicked him in the stomach, and caught him with a right hook that lifted him into the air and sent him flying back down the steps. His head hit the ground with a simultaneous thud and crack. Spotty went back inside and slammed the door.

It was some time before Danny told him that the insurance man was still there, and that blood was oozing from his head. They called the emergency service, but Mr. McCormack died from his hemorrhage three days later. His luck had been changed.

At the trial it turned out that Mr. McCormack had an adopted daughter, now well into her twenties. That had surprised Spotty; he hadn't imagined the man behind the mask. He had been truly moved by the sight of McCormack's widow and adopted daughter attending the viewings, two dark ghosts hit by falling marbles. But he had no remorse for Matti; the man had decided to wear the mask. It let no-one see in, but it was a two-way mask and it had prevented him from seeing beyond it, too. 'Like a high wall, Bro, built so they can't see in, but it means you can't see out either, you get that?'

Ambrose thought about the prison then, and the simile confused him. 'Those on one side can't see the others, right?'

Even more curious was the fact that Matti McCormack had an elderly mother – in a wheelchair! She had fallen down the steps at the local library and shattered her hip. Her son had taken the council to court and was granted generous indemnification. He was in the trade. It took Spotty years of reflection to understand that this was circumstantial evidence and had no real bearing on the case in hand; it was nothing more than a 'philosophical red herring', as he put it. Ambrose nodded.

'You know who the really lucky ones are?'

He stared at Ambrose, though both of them knew that the answer, if there was one, would be supplied by Spotty himself.

'Well it ain't me and it ain't you, right?'

Ambrose laughed. That meant that his friend needed a break, wanted to snap out of it for a few minutes. He would return to the topic sooner or later, but for now he wanted to change the subject. Perhaps it was a cue, the perfect moment to raise his own issue, to talk about what he had come for.

'How are the … the plans… coming on? Have you 'ironed them out' yet?'

Spotty smiled. It was time to have a bit of fun with his old pal Bro.

'What you got in the bag? Eh, what's in the bag, let me see. Put the things on the table, let's have a look at them.'

Then he saw it, the puzzled look he enjoyed so much. Ambrose was trying desperately to figure out why on earth he should empty his few mundane belongings on to Myra's kitchen table. Why would Spotty want to have a look at them? What could possibly be of interest in such everyday objects? It never occurred to him that he was being taken for a ride, being ridiculed, being laughed at. No matter how many times you did things like that to Bro, he never clicked, never for a moment doubted your sincerity. Poor fool.

'Well, there's not much here, really. A shaver, Phillips, ….'

'Stop! I don't give a fuck what's in your bag, Bro. They're your things, your personal belongings. Keep them to yourself, or for your next of kin. You've got no business showing them to anyone, not even me, right? Try and remember that. Nobody. O.k.?'

Spotty looked irritated. He was angry with Ambrose because Ambrose never learnt his lessons, or if he did, then he learnt them too slowly. How many times had he told him to keep his dignity? How often had he warned him about people taking advantage of him? Ambrose noticed it and tried to make amends.

'OK, I just thought you wanted to have a look. I don't mind. There's nothing …..'

But Spotty cut him short, stopped him in his tracks.

'I got the final contact. All I need to do is make a few phone calls.'

He couldn't avoid playing cat and mouse with Ambrose; it was too tempting, too easy. From the moment they had met Spotty had noticed the lost expression on Ambrose's face. It was the look of someone who didn't understand what was going on, but who had come to terms with that. He had never understood, so it was second nature. Ambrose Ork. With a name like that was it any wonder? He had been dealt the worst hand, the low numbers, and didn't even have the intelligence to bluff, or hold his cards to his chest. He was the typical idiot who would show them to whoever asked to see them. A loser. Worse. A born loser. Others were born with aces stashed away up every sleeve, or knew how to make you think they had even if they hadn't. But Ork was always going to lose one way or another, because he set himself up for it. He said 'here I am, fool me, trick me, I won't even realize it so don't bother your conscience too much over that.'

Spotty had joined in the fun at first and made a scapegoat of him. There was always one, often more than one, who was needed to run errands, to do the chores nobody else wanted to do. Someone to dupe, someone you knew would swallow every absurd lie and tall tale, someone who could be turned into collateral damage if necessary.

But Ambrose was different because he was innocent. By that

Spotty didn't mean 'not guilty', that was another matter altogether. He meant that Ambrose was innocent the way children are innocent, because he had no malice. He had no malice because he could never be sure that the fault was not his, could so easily be led to believe that it was slow-off-the-mark Ambrose Ork who should be asking for forgiveness. Which did not turn him into a saint, either. He could get angry like the rest of them, over meals, over someone taking his things. He could be bad-mannered, foul-mouthed, foul-minded. But there was no malice, and Spotty had recognized that.

That, and the fact that he was a great listener.

So little by little Richard 'Spotty' Dodd had taken Ambrose under his wing. He became his protector, and kept him from coming to too much harm. In return Ambrose would listen and nod, often with his mouth just a little open, while Spotty exercised his genius.

Spotty had met many like Bro in his time. They were the coat-holders, the street sweepers, the uncomplaining doormat of humanity. He had worked beside them in factories, punching out ball bearings so that the likes of Mr. Haute could live in luxury, in lofty warehouses pushing the dust from shelf to shelf, on hot, dry roads as the tarmac poured out, on dredgers in murky canals. There was no romance in them. They were like everybody else, some of them were sullen, some clowns, others were violent, or timid. The only difference was that they seemed to work on a different timescale, as if they lived in slow motion, the way an elephant or a Galapagos tortoise would live. Bradypsychia the nurses and doctors called it at the prison hospital. They knew that two plus two plus two makes six, but take their own sweet time to reach that conclusion. They make you want to finish their sentences for them because you know what they are going to say long before they have even reached half way. In short, thick. Thick as a brick, thick as two short planks.

He himself had been confused for one of them by that insurance man. MCormack had assumed that, being poor, Spotty was therefore a fool, a blunt tool. Now he was dead. One more less of the bastards.

Why was that? What was the difference? Because Spotty had fought back. That was the worst of the dimwits; they just take things as they are, never complaining, just getting on with it like beasts of burden. Well nothing is gained by conformity. For a few months in prison Spotty had run a section called Thought of the Day. It had been an attempt at sparking a little debate, but had eventually been taken over by the religious elements, who began to cover the notice board in glib biblical quotations about succour and redemption. So he had abandoned the idea. Spotty preferred a more rebellious line, and one of his favourites had been 'A slave is one who waits for someone to free him', by Ezra Pound. Not that he had ever read Pound, or Nietzsche, or Socrates. He was not interested in the buildup, only the conclusion, the crystallized philosophy. Don't be a slave. Fight back. How he had tried to beat that into Ambrose's thick head. To no avail, of course. Ambrose did not see himself as a slave, and knew the date of his release. So what was Spotty on about?

It was frustrating the way he refused to help himself.

'There are two contacts who are going to help us out on this. You don't need to know who the first one is, that's all taken care of and the less you know the better.'

He stared at Ambrose as if to make sure he was still awake, still paying attention. Ambrose nodded.

'You don't need to know any more than that your friend Spotty has sorted it all out.'

Time for a little more praise.

'And you thought I'd forget!'

'No, no, I was sure you'd be there, I knew it, I was sure.'

Ambrose was about to go into a typical, heartfelt gratitude speech, using phrases he had picked up during his life, platitudes mostly as he was not prone to originality, but Spotty would not give him the satisfaction. He wanted to remain just a touch hurt, to wallow in self-pity for a while just for the hell of it. It was the best way to stay one step ahead of them all. Pretend, give a false impression, hold something back, keep them guessing.

'O.k., o.k., don't start getting all sincere on me, for fuck's sake. I'm doing it for you because you're like a brother to me. Bro, eh?'

He struck his chest with his fist.

'I'm doing this for you, Bro, I don't get anything out of this but trouble, big trouble. That's why I don't want you to know any more than is strictly necessary. Modus operandi. Incognito.'

He winked and chuckled to himself. He could be a bastard at times.

Still there was an element of truth in everything he said. He was indeed helping Ambrose for no ulterior motive. He was taking risks too, even though he was sure they were minimal. The most he could stand to make out of the whole deal was a word of thanks, and maybe a cut from the car dealers, though that was by no means assured; they were shifty customers. The worst he could expect it was better not to dwell on.

'Thanks, thanks.'

Ambrose was lost for words. He grinned.

'You're the boss, you're the best.'

He realized that sounded stupid, but it was the best he could do.

'Shut up and give me a cigarette.'

They smoked, seriously, the way others fiddle with rosary beads. Every so often the fridge jumped to life, competing for a time with the electric sounds of the table fan, but it didn't have the necessary stamina and soon fell silent again. The sun's rays now came in slanted through the glass panels of the back door, picking out the rising smoke like the light from a projector at an old fashioned cinema. The day was gradually fading though the heat remained, as heavy and sticky as guilt.

The whole plan was Spotty's idea; everything was Spotty's idea. He had heard Ambrose's unlikely tale, had quizzed him over and over again until he was convinced of its truth. Then he had started to make his plan. Why? That was a question not even Spotty could have answered clearly, let alone Ambrose. There had been so many long chats about the reasons behind his friend's interest in the case that Ambrose had long given up any hope of understanding anything except the barest bones of the final plan. How could he possibly keep track of all that high level philosophy? They had talked about, correction, *Spotty* had talked about, revenge, justice, punishment, remorse. Restoring the balance. Something about cold dishes and settling scores, a lot of new words whose meaning he had felt too embarrassed to ask about. On and on, mixing it all up, going all over it again but in a different sequence, rambling, reaching conclusions that were always only temporary. Now all this stuff about luck again, and whether it was good or bad or in between; it was enough to baffle anyone. One thing was clear, though; Spotty had taken on Ambrose's cause as if it were his own.

And the plan was a good one, water-tight and carefully put together.

'When are you thinking of doing this, then?'

'Soon as possible?'

'That's up to you, Bro, that's up to you. Ready when you are.'

'And those phone calls? They alright?'

'Ready when you are.'

Spotty should have wound it up then, it was his cue. But he had not finished yet.

'Remember- the luckiest are those who make no noise, attract no attention to themselves, who glide from birth to death without too much success or tragedy.'

Was this advice? Was he trying to warn Ambrose about something? Or was he back to his philosophising again?

'They complain about how boring life is, how they never had any adventure. "Never seen a dead body" they say, as if that were something to look forward to. Never been in trouble, never had to steal or beg, never had a really bad accident. Never won the lottery and had my kids kidnapped. So they watch those shitty soap operas and dramas and stuff, and cry their eyes out for those others they see, so much suffering, so much pain. But it never happens to them. And instead of feeling lucky and thanking god, they feel that they've missed out on something, for fuck's sake. "We want tragedy! " Well they are the lucky ones, Bro.'

So he had wanted to clear that up, make his final comment. That was fine by Ambrose.

'You're right, Spotty.'

'Of course I'm fucking right. I'm *always* right, right?'

'Right.'

'Well as long as we all agree on that… Let's make a couple of calls.'

5

Harvey had taken over one of the ground floor rooms for himself. He was never sure if it was now his study, somewhere cosy and personal, or his office, a place where work is done and decisions are made. The walls were lined with books, as were a number of rooms in the house, and the furniture was extremely old world. The writing desk was huge and heavy, and shone with a dull, dark brown light. The chairs were also sturdy, cushioned, straight backed affairs as if they had been picked up from a notary's office. And despite the large windows, the ceiling lights, and the many corner lamps, a residual darkness still lurked around the huge oil paintings and along the skirting boards. So to cheer the place up, to modernise it, to leave his mark, Harvey had added a large, leather, ultra modern executive swivel chair, a glass and stainless steel side desk cluttered with all the latest technological advances, and by the door a water dispenser, clear and cool, exactly like the one in his city office. He offered a tiny, inverted cone of spring water to Joe Stein, who declined the offer. Ambrose? There was a moment's hesitation as Ambrose searched for Stein's advice, which was not forthcoming. So he took one and swallowed it in a gulp. Then, unsure what to do with the paper cup, he decided to screw it up and pop it in his pocket. Harvey tossed his into a waste paper bin specifically placed by the dispenser for such occasions. But no comment was made, so Ambrose relaxed again.

As Stein by now knew, Mr. Paulson had a plan. He had first mentioned it some months back, but since then Harvey had done his homework and the project was now, as he had put it, 'mature'. So he had called for Joe Stein and Ambrose to meet him in his office, or study, so that he could go over the details with them, in detail. He suggested they take a chair each. So they sat, perfectly erect, as if sitting to attention, whilst Harvey leant back in his chair and swivelled, looking at them from across his chest.

'Now I've given this a lot of thought and it's something I, we, have been meaning to do for some time.'

He paused here, as if he expected either Stein or Ambrose to interject, but neither of them did, so he continued.

'I spoke to you about this a few months back, Mr. Stein, about the layout and the design. Well since then I've been in touch with a number of specialised firms, some more specialised than others!'

A little joke that he was happy to see raised a smile on Stein's face. Ambrose hadn't picked up on it. Typical. Enough humour, back to business.

'Anyway, after sifting through god knows how many brochures, quotes.... and after deciding exactly what we want done, we have decided it is time to put the plan into action. So that we can get started and hopefully have it all finished by the time the good weather arrives.'

Mr. Stein nodded his agreement. Ambrose followed suit.

'I assume that so far you have not discussed this with anyone?'

Stein was under orders not to do so. He confirmed that the secret was indeed still a secret.

'Right Ambrose, let me fill you in. What I want is to re-do the entire pool area. Most of the flagstones are cracked, the showers look as if they were built before the war, the benches are old and buckled.....'

He waved his hands about and grimaced as if to say 'a disaster, unfit for us'.

Ambrose, unsure what to do, did nothing.

'It's going to cost quite a lot of money, but it is something that has to be done, not only for us, but for visitors and guests. We can hardly throw a barbecue or a pool party with a pool like that, now can we?'

Another little joke, another smile from Stein. Ambrose was beginning to feel left out.

'It's out of date, run down, ugly, and....'

He let the sentence fade out as he realised he could not state here that the whole pool area stank of the past, of the Haute family, of bygone days that no longer concerned him. He wanted to rip out the last vestiges of that dynasty and start afresh. Andrea was with him on this. They had to turn Haute House into *their* home. To do so, they had to redecorate, redesign, and bring the place into line with their generation. The master of the house is dead; long live the master of the house.

'The pool itself will be retiled. Andrea has already chosen the colours and the logo. The rest of the area will be ripped up, entirely, all of it, from the terrace steps down to the garden path, and as far as the flower beds. Wooden boarding will be placed around the pool, with sunken lights built in, and a row of lampposts will be strung around that, demarking the pool zone from the other zones. The benches will go, the old stonework will go, the showers will be replaced by modern units with push button controls. I had wanted to acclimatise the pool, too, but having studied the various offers and options have decided against it. I have marked.....'

He leant across his desk and pulled over a plan of the pool area.

'...some power points, here, here, here, here, and here, once again imbedded into the woodwork, but readily available should they be needed. Music, ice machine, cleaning tools and whatever.'

He did not show the plan to either Stein or Ambrose, but just kept it to himself, jabbing at it here and there with his pen as if talking to himself.

'If we get started right away we should be fine. Ideally I want all this done by the end of May. The specialised work we will have to... farm it out.... get an outside firm to come in and do that part, naturally, but a lot of it we can do on our own. Pulling out the old stuff, preparing the terrain, getting it all ready for when they turn up. And, and this is the part I want you to pay special attention to, Ambrose.'

On hearing his name he seemed to start, as if he had just snapped out of some kind of reverie or other.

'Are you up to it, eh? Do you realise what I'm saying here, Ambrose?'

No.

'I mean, once the worst of it has been dug up and thrown out. What's next? What then, eh Ambrose?'

It was a habit he had fallen into without realising it. Harvey would ask Ambrose these questions, knowing full well that the poor man had no idea what to respond. It was something he did instinctively. Ambrose raised his shoulders. How could he possibly know if it was all a secret?

'The electrical fittings! The wiring! You up to that, Ambrose? It's a big job – the boarding, the little lamps and power points, the new lampposts. Not the pool lights, they'll need specialist installation, but the rest... Do you think you can do it? Are you our man?'

Ambrose stole a quick glance at Stein, who had opened his eyes just a little, just enough for Ambrose to realise that it was now time to confirm. Without a doubt. Yes, sir.

'Yes, Mr Paulson. No problem, sir.'

Harvey examined Ambrose and was not convinced. Throughout the monologue Ambrose had appeared like a man who was being washed off deck by a storm of unretainable information. His eyes shifted, because he had never been able to hold

Harvey's gaze. Why not? Was he shy? Or was it that he was afraid of being caught out, an impostor pretending to understand and follow the conversation? Or maybe he did not like being treated like a fool, maybe he had taken offence. Was he about to make a comment, or would he just sit there and stare back blankly? His mouth hung open, not too much, but enough for any neutral observer to affirm that Ambrose Ork certainly *looked* gormless, even if he wasn't.

'You sure? You're not going to let me down on this? You are sure you're qualified to undertake this... '

The word eluded Harvey, or rather the only one that sprang to mind was 'undertaking', so he trailed off.

'I'm sure he can manage, Mr. Paulson, his father was a fine teacher. Right Bro?'

Ambrose smiled at that.

'Yes. No problem, sir. No problem.'

Harvey smiled too.

'So be it, then. Mr. Stein, if you have a minute or two I'd like to go over the plans with you so that you can then fill Ambrose in with the finer details.'

'Of course.'

Ambrose didn't move.

'I'll talk to you later. Lunchtime'

He finally understood Joe's cue, and took his leave.

Harvey frowned at Stein.

'He'll be fine. He's better than you think.'

'He didn't understand a word'.

'He'll be alright, I'll explain it all to him in detail later. He just needs a little time to assimilate it, that's all. He'll be fine.'

Harvey shook his head in disbelief.

'How on earth did he get a job here? I really can't understand how they ever took him on.'

Stein did not like such comments, even though he was used to them by now. It wasn't so much that he didn't agree with Harvey's assessment of Ambrose and his ability to perform certain functions. They all had a giggle at Bro's antics at some time or other. But coming from Harvey.... It became malicious, malicious gossip. There was no humour intended, only criticism. Mr. Paulson did not like Ambrose, had no real affection for him, not at all. He just wanted to ridicule and jibe and insult the man, regardless of his feelings. It was true; Ambrose was more than hopeless at times. But the household had come to feel for him over the years, and Joe did not think it right that this Harvey, whom nobody cared for in the slightest, should take it upon himself to talk behind his back, to mock him and sneer at his incompetence. Because it was not Ambrose's fault that he had been born a bit slow off the mark. To blame him for that was like trying to blame someone for having big ears, or poor eyesight. It was not right, not the done thing.

Malicious gossip. He'd just about had enough of it, having suffered it himself for years. Joe Stein was whatever people imagined him to be in their ignorance. He was not married, so he must be gay, probably had a man friend tucked away somewhere. Or maybe he was having an affair with Señora Luz. The very idea scandalised him, not because he could not bear to be coupled with Luz albeit in an imaginary world. No, that was not a problem. The problem was that Señora Luz had her own intimacy, her own inner world that had to be respected. By insinuating that he was having an affair with her, they also insinuated that *she* was having an affair with *him*. Intolerable. He knew that rumour had once had it that he had been sleeping with Alice Haute! The Alice that everyone assumed was a snooty, high and mighty lady of the house, when she had been no more than a very good actress. Kind, caring, discreet, and eventually crushed by cruel fate. He had to put in a good word for Ambrose and cut Harvey short.

'He's a good worker, and a very good electrician. He knows what he's doing, he's a good man. He'll be fine, just fine.'

Harvey half sniffed, half smiled. He would gladly have continued criticising Ambrose, but Mr. Stein was so...so.... Stern? Stern Stein. And difficult to fathom. Harvey had never been able to work out just what it was about Stein that he didn't like, that he didn't trust. There was so much about him that he didn't know, such a long history of service stretching back to when Arnold Haute had still been alive, when Sydney was no bigger than his son was now. How many secrets did he keep behind those rimless glasses, how many loyalties did he still maintain? Stein knew so much but gave away so little that Harvey couldn't conclude if he were extremely reserved or extremely deceitful. He had pushed him and probed him over the last couple of years, but Stein had come out as immaculate as ever, always in control, always in his place, his feathers forever unruffled. Was he a closet gay? Did he have a mistress somewhere, perhaps on another estate? Was there any truth in the rumours about him and the late Mrs Haute? Probably not; people talk too much about things that do not concern them, especially in small, closed societies. Still, through his manner and his insistence on Ambrose's capabilities he had made it clear that today they were not going to get a laugh at the fool's expense. Pity, but so be it.

Harvey explained everything in minute detail to Stein, emphasising the most important points, underlining and ringing certain words or figures. He wanted to be exhaustive because he was about to delegate, to hand over to Joe Stein the whole plan. Naturally, as the mastermind and financer of the scheme he was still the overall boss, and the final word was indisputably his. But for the day to day business, Stein was to become the overseer, the site manager. Which meant that if all went well,

Harvey was to be congratulated, but that any snags or delays were down to Stein's inability to see the job through to a successful conclusion. The chain of command. Pass it on.

Joe Stein closed the door behind him as well as he could with his arms full of folders and rolled up plans. He was hoping it wouldn't slam, as that would give the wrong impression, but pulling it to with his elbow was an uncertain science. Luckily it clicked gently into place.

It was a good idea. The pool really could have done with an overhaul long ago, it was tacky and falling to pieces, and Harvey certainly didn't do things by halves. Embedded lighting, swanky new showers, decking. It would look great once the wood was down. The upkeep would be a chore, as maintaining decking throughout the year was a time consuming task, but it would be worth it in the end. Anyway, it wouldn't be *him* who got down on his knees and treated the wood. He laughed as he imagined Ambrose slogging away. But the best part was that it would probably be the staff that got most use out of it, especially during the week. But...

Later, looking back, he would not be able to put into words what he had felt back then. It wasn't anything concrete, nothing he could put his finger on and say 'that was it'. No, it was more like a nagging doubt that something was not right. He sounded more like Pet, he knew, and forever held his silence even to the police. You had to be serious with people like that. They worked on evidence, not hearsay or hunches. But he had definitely come out of that interview with Harvey with a strange sensation in his guts. No more than that, but no less either. The question he would ask himself throughout his retirement years was whether he remembered that uneasy feeling solely because of what later happened. Was he going back and colouring in, adding details in retrospect that in reality had never existed? Could he trust himself and his memory to respect, in a neutral way, the true sequence of events, or was he inevitably bound to edit, to rediscover, to elaborate? He often felt that the present cast a shadow over the past, making it difficult to discern its contours in detail. So torches and floodlights were called in, only to create the same distorting effect.

Yet there was something about Harvey's manner, about the way he had pored over those plans and prepared everything with so much detail and care, that made Joe Stein feel wary. Harvey was not usually so intent on Ambrose carrying out a specific task, did not normally confide in him. That was not how things worked. The most natural way was to first let Stein know what had to be done, then wait for results. He had stopped talking directly to Ambrose some time back now, when he had decided that the letter from the lawyer was enough. So why had he called *both* of them into his study when one, Joe himself, would have served the same purpose? And why this sudden change in attitude, not only towards Ambrose, but towards the whole lot of them, little Sydney included? Because it was as clear as day that Harvey hated the kid, couldn't bring himself to so much as hug him, let alone spend time with him, play with him. Now he would even seek him out, for Pete's sake. Well maybe there had been a change of heart, maybe there was no real mystery at all, maybe Harvey was just mellowing and settling in to his new life. Perhaps if nothing had ever happened Joe would have accepted this swing in attitude as something relatively common, nothing out of the ordinary. But in context...

Back outside Harvey's study cum office he simply felt slightly surprised at the curious interview, not worried or perplexed in any way, but aware that from somewhere in his head a voice advised caution. He should have paid more attention to that at the time.

Joe Stein had to hand it to Harvey – he was an excellent organiser. All the ground work had been done, and all Stein had to do now was act as overseer. Harvey had studied the quotes, choosing the firms not only by cost but also on their ability to get the job done on time. They would start with the pool. It would be completely gutted and retiled before anything else.

Once that had been done, the surrounding area would be totally redesigned, the electrical wiring put down, and the plumbing for the showers laid out, so that the final installation would be the wooden decking. Harvey had worked out the schedule to the day. Mr. Paulson would be in charge of the payments, too, which was a relief, as that part often turned ugly, especially if the workmanship was shoddy and the final result not what the customer had imagined.

Two weeks later a team of workers arrived at the break of dawn and began stripping out the old pool. Ambrose was dragged in to help out with the less popular chores. They brought winches and planks and pneumatic drills, wheelbarrows and skips, pick axes, chisels and huge shovels. Vans and lorries came and went at all hours, and clouds of semi invisible dust headed straight for the house, creeping in under doors and through minute cracks, covering everything in a fine layer of earthy talc. Luz and Pet did their best and cursed the day that Harvey had decided to bring in the builders, while Andrea stayed on her side of the house, luckily far from the noise and dirt of the site itself.

Where today she was enjoying one those rare occasions when life suddenly makes sense, when time is suspended and you are rewarded for an immortal moment with what you consider to be heaven on earth. Still in her pyjamas, her face unwashed, her hair hanging loose over her shoulders, she was half sitting, half lying on the sofa, her feet tucked up, one arm on the rest, cradling her son. Sydney lay still in her arms, breathing gently, almost imperceptibly, his face turned up towards her, his eyes closed. The fingers of his tiny hand stroked her forearm every so often, casually, caressingly. The only sound was that of the birds singing in the garden, and of a distant vacuum cleaner which seemed to rock them with its rhythmical movements. It was Saturday, and there would be no noisy workers today. The light that fell in through the huge windows behind them was elegant and perfectly suited to the scene. The room was still, mother and child fused as one in peace and human warmth. She would have to try and catch it while it lasted, before Sydney started to fidget, before his gentle stroking turned into sticky, annoying scratching, before he began to kick at her and demand some other type of attention. Because these cameos were very rare indeed, Sydney hardly ever sitting still for more than a few minutes at a time. He didn't require much physical contact, getting along just fine with a short hug, a couple of hasty kisses, so the fact that he should be lying so quietly in her lap, so docile and snug, was something she had to make the most of. She would do her best to soak it all up, to drain every last drop, to burn the moment into her memory cells, hoping that by so doing she could make it last forever. Like a mental photograph to be added to her album. Or maybe video clip would be a better description, as most of her memories lasted at least a few seconds. She had quite a few by now. Riding on the back of her father's motorbike in the snow, hugging his ice cold leather jacket, feeling the tyres slip and slide under her as she gripped with all the young strength of her thighs. Mother at work, the table strewn with papers and artwork in an orderly mess only she could understand. The look on Aylissa's face when she had surprised her by kissing her on the mouth. That had been daredevil, purposefully provocative, but it had gone no further than that, and now they never mentioned it in words, although it was permanently present between them. And Sydney of course. So many of him, some kind, some funny. Caring for his mother when she was down with 'flu, or fooling around in a hotel room with the towels. But there were a number of crueller snapshots, too. One of them particularly terrible; the look of fear and disappointment when she had told him she was pregnant. It had flitted across his features so fast that he even tried to bluff his way out of it. 'That's fantastic, Andrea!' But she had spotted it, his initial reaction, and it hurt. And it hurt even more when he turned on the smile and the flashing teeth. So cynical. So false.

She looked down at their son. The same slightly narrow eyes, the same fair hair, the generous lips and cleft chin. He would grow up to be a handsome young charmer just like his father, she thought. A door slammed and Sydney groaned. This would not last much longer now, the precious moments in life being always so brief.

Life is a bully, she concluded. Things are fine when he's looking the other way, but the instant he decides to pick on you again, there is nothing you can do. He knocks your father out with one blow, then sends your mother off with a lunatic intent on visiting every damned corner of the globe. Then, magnanimous, he introduces you to Sydney Haute, the most eligible bachelor of them all. Come, he says, try this glass of champagne. Only to punch you in the stomach at your first sip so that you spill the drink and throw up on the spot. She had been bullied into widowhood, bullied into single parenthood, bullied into being the heiress of a fortune that she had neither sought nor desired. Now here she was, remarried to the ambiguous Harvey, sitting on a sofa in her pyjamas and cuddling her fatherless son, surrounded by wealth and luxury, hoping to immortalise a few seconds of peace and tranquillity.

'Scratch me. Here, on my shoulder.'

Sydney was shaking off his lethargy. Andrea did as she was told.

'Higher. To the left. The left! No, not there, lower down. Harder! You're not doing it right! Scratch me!'

She pushed him away. It was over. He would soon start demanding and negotiating, forever raising the stakes until she snapped at him or capitulated. Or both, probably.

'I'm hungry.'

He said it as an accusation, as if his mother had neglected him.

'You've just had your breakfast. You'll have to wait a little bit, not long, just until Pet comes round.'

'I'm hungry now. I don't want to have to wait, not for *her*. She hates me!'

That was untrue, as both of them knew, and said only to jolt Andrea into action or reaction. As always she rose to the bait.

'Don't say that about Auntie Pet, it's not true and it's not fair. She loves you, we all love you, nobody hates you.'

'*She* does.'

'She does not, it's nonsense.'

She passed the back of her hand over her brow wearily. This was tiresome, but she had no idea how to put a stop to it. She knew others, Pet and Luz among them, but also friends and relatives, that never suffered these tirades, always knew exactly what to say or do to cut the little bastards short. But Andrea had not been brought up to mother children. She had been brought up to be pampered, just like her son, and she hadn't the slightest notion of how to handle the situation. Andrea had become pregnant as the logical consequence of getting married. It was something she had looked forward to as a milestone in her life, like losing her virginity. She was quite prepared to give birth; it was part of her role as a woman. Becoming a competent mother was a different story.

What she wanted was for Sydney to grow up, preferably quickly, so that she could reason with him and ask him if he felt it was right to criticise those who cared for him and loved him. She could ask him if he didn't feel he was being just a tad unreasonable. Because in reality he wasn't even hungry. And he thought the world of Pet. So did he behave that way as some kind of form of punishment towards her? Blaming her for his father's death, perhaps? Surely he could see that that was unfair. But the boy was only five, and he had no intention of quitting, or listening to abstract arguments. He would cry and scream and demand simply because he could, because he was allowed to, because it suited him.

'I'm hungry. I'm going to get some chocolate.'

She had to pull him back by his arm. He glared at her as if to say 'how dare you touch me?' He tried to pull himself away.

'I'm hungry, I'm hungry, I'm hungry. I want some chocolate. Let me go, let me go!'

She had to assert her authority.

'That's enough! I don't want another word from you, do you hear? That's enough, you can have some chocolate when Pet comes.'

The boy sensed victory.

'But that might take ages.'

'Not until Pet comes round. It won't be long now. Just sit and wait, there's a good boy.'

'But she might not come.'

'Don't be silly, she always comes just after eleven.'

'The other day she didn't.'

Andrea could not remember if this was true or not. She thought it was probably not, but did not dare to call his bluff. Her memory was not to be trusted at the best of times.

'She'll be along soon, you'll see.'

He stopped trying to escape and looked up at her with puppy dog eyes.

'I'm hungry now, Mum.'

Just like his father, she thought, but it worked nonetheless.

'Well alright, just a tiny bit. But you have to promise me you won't say that about Auntie Pet again, ok? Do you promise?'

'Promise',

and he was off to the cupboard where the sweets were kept.

Pet arrived just after eleven with milk and biscuits. Plain

biscuits that Sydney all but tossed to the floor in disdain. He would maybe take a wee sip of milk, maybe. Pet threw a glance at Andrea, who sighed heavily, but smiled too, as if saying that everything was fine as far as she was concerned, and as she was the mother, that ought to be enough for anyone. Pet sat down on the sofa next to Andrea and pinched a biscuit.

'If he doesn't want his biscuits, I do.'

'Hey, they're mine!'

He lunged for the biscuit.

'A-a. Not anymore. You're not hungry, remember?'

And she scoffed it down. Sydney smiled at Pet, enjoying the game, and picked up a biscuit himself.

'And drink up your milk before I have it too, I'm *starving*!'

He leapt to the coffee table where Pet had placed the glass of milk and threatened to down it in one gulp.

'Go on, then! That'll make you big and strong, eh, Mum?'

Andrea realised she was being shown how it was done, but did not appreciate the interference. It was criticism more than advice, she perceived. Well if Pet was such a good mother, although she did not have any children herself, at least not that anyone knew of, well then she could look after the little shit for a while. She searched for an excuse, something more convincing than just passing the buck, but then decided against having to explain herself to Pet or Sydney or anyone at all. Why should she have to? She simply wanted to be alone for a while.

'Can you stay with Auntie Pet for a bit, Sydney?'

But that sounded too abrupt, so she added,

'I have to get ready.'

And waltzed out of the room without looking back.

Which was fine with Pet; she preferred to be left alone with her young charge, that way she could treat him as she felt fit without having to worry about whether Mum would agree or not. She had built up quite a relationship with the boy over the years and really felt like she was his Auntie Pet. He was her nephew, or her younger cousin, or family of some kind, because they had spent so many hours together and knew each other so well. Ever since Sydney had been able to half understand her, that is from about six months on, Pet had laid down the law, had drawn him her very simple but also very well defined lines. The boy knew better than to cross them, although he was tempted to test them every so often to make sure there had been no change or development. She could admonish him now with a slight hissing through her teeth. Be good, Sydney, or face the consequences, it's up to you. He understood her perfectly.

He needed a brother. The poor kid spent so many moments on his own, not knowing what to do with himself, having to turn to adults for fun and companionship, adults who usually had no time for such infantile activity. What was it with the rich, she often asked herself, that they only have one child at a time? The late Sydney Haute, the only son. Andrea, no sisters or brothers. Harvey, the spoilt brat, brought up all on his own. Did they have children just because it was expected of them, like kings and queens of old? Someone to leave it all to, an heir to the throne? Because they certainly didn't seem to love their offspring very much. They were always too keen to get someone else to bring them up for them. Someone to change their nappies, someone to take them for walks, someone to play with them. Then they sent them away to school or summer camps, or kept them busy with monitors and tutors. More like keeping dogs than starting a family. And now this little chap, once again all on his lonesome.

'Help me with this, and we can go and see Uncle Bro with the dogs. Come on.'

Sydney carried his plate down the corridors to the kitchen, trotting behind Pet like a duckling behind its mother.

Of course, there was always hope. Maybe Harvey and Andrea would seal their relationship with one of their own, that way giving Sid a playmate, albeit a bit late in the game. Yet somehow Pet couldn't see it happening. It was not easy to say why, but that was not important. She just could not imagine it, and that was usually enough. Andrea had been a reluctant mother right from the start. How could she want to be a mother when that meant sacrifice and unconditional love? Not exactly up Andrea's street. Nor Sydney's, the father's, either. They were far too used to having everything done for them to want to get bogged down pretending to be caring parents. Luckily they had her, and Luz and Bro to fall back on. Not Joe, though, he kept his hands well clean he did. No, no kids for Mr. Stein!

Pet would have made a fairly decent mother most people agreed, but she was not so sure. Firstly, she did not like to cut people up into different categories. He's a good husband, or she's a wonderful friend. No, you either were or you weren't *everything*. Maybe she had picked that up off her father, how he had not wanted to say that he was no more than his professional status, but it was an opinion she held strongly. You are a good mother because you love children, and are able to put others before yourself. In *all* cases. It was a natural conclusion to being how you really are, not having to fake it or try too hard to be like how others want you to be. If you were just *natural*, that's all. And Pet was not the marrying type, so raising a family became, if not impossible then at least more difficult. She was not the marrying type because she liked men. Not one type of man, she had no preconceived preference, couldn't care less if they were dark or fair, tall or short, fat or slim, just as long as something clicked between them. They would come into her life almost by accident, and more often than not leave in the same way. There was nothing planned, and she preferred it that way. There had been married men, life-long bachelors, passers through, and the odd one who had quite simply grasped at the opportunity to get his end away without a fuss. She never demanded anything in return, it was all here and now and the devil be damned, tomorrow is another day stuff. Naturally she could not entertain at the House, but even that suited her, too. Pet made love in the toilets of quiet bars, in the backs of enormous lorries, in a telephone booth under the shade of trees. She enjoyed quick gropes under snack bar tables or in the last row of the cinema. It was clandestine and naughty, and so much better than those awkward hotel room scenes, where you both undress embarrassedly and slip under the sheets like nervous novices. Here I am, undressed for the part. We shall now practice mutual sex. I am ready. It was all too mechanical and only served to put her off the whole idea. How much more exciting to ride the moment, to let the lust surge, to brush and suggest until it was unbearable. Now, here and now, and who gives a shit if they catch us! So finding a man and marrying him, and setting up a stable home, with children and the whole works was not going to happen, was not in her nature. No matter, she had Sydney to pretend with. And Bro to look after too, of course. And what man would put up with her *and* Bro, eh? Not an attractive proposition. Still, it was not up to her to question her destiny. Things were as they were, and there was no point fighting it. But Sydney would grow up an only child, of that she was sure.

Later, before the mirror, Andrea reminded herself that she did not need to justify her actions, or her opinions for that matter, to anyone. She was a free and independent woman who made her own decisions, followed her own criteria. Nobody had the right to judge her, to criticise, or to force their own moral values on her. Andrea didn't need any of that, thank you; she was quite capable of thinking for herself. She gave herself a confirming nod. Too bloody right. But the truth was, as she realised whilst pursing her lips for the lipstick, that she was feeling a tiny bit repentant for having thought badly of Pet. Yes, she was fat and ugly, and smoked all the time, forever slipping off to have a quick cigarette, blowing the smoke out of the toilet window. She waddled rather than walked, and was constantly out of breath. What else? Her teeth! Tombstones set in dried blood.

Which was a shame, because otherwise she had a sweet smile. Because Pet *was* sweet. She was not bright, or witty, or even crafty. No, she was more like her brother when it came to mental agility, but somehow she was endearing. Pet hadn't been criticising her, she now understood. She wasn't like that. She was sweet, sweet natured, and kind too. Pet thought the world of little Sydney, she knew, and was only trying to help. Because despite her many faults, Pet was, deep down, and sincerely, a good woman. By good Andrea meant that she was not bad, that in Pet there was a lack of desire to do harm. Perhaps, unintentionally, she might hurt your feelings, or tread on your toes, or wake up grumpy and foul-mouthed, but when the chips were down, Pet, just like her brother, was submissive. How they both accepted their lot without complaint was to be admired, was something that maybe others might even learn from. Andrea imagined then a windy street, with icy blasts, and poor Pet waiting at the bus stop for the bus to arrive. But when it did, it was so full of people that it just swept past, leaving her freezing cold on the pavement. What should she do? Wait for the next bus, or start walking home? Either way she knew Pet would be alright, would eventually get home, and think no more of it. She was a good woman, and it had not been right to think what she had thought about her being a spinster, a motherless, unmarried, unattractive, middle-aged cook cum cleaner. That had been unfair, even if there was a germ of truth in it.

Yes. Pet was sweet and good, and meant no harm to anyone. Could she say the same about herself, or about Harvey, come to that? Was there malice in Harvey? She checked her skin, scouring the surface of her face for blemishes. He was hard-nosed, they said, a hard-nosed business man. Was that the same? Could that be classed 'bad'? In a way it was a trait she rather respected, the ability to get on in life like that. Thick-skinned. But it instils fear, too, in a way, his cold-hearted approach to others. Thank god he seemed to have eased up a bit on the home front, because he had been unnecessarily hard on poor Ambrose, on all of them, but especially on Bro. That was unfair; it was like picking on somebody younger or smaller than yourself. Luckily he had he had stopped all that; it was leading to nowhere, and just made life that much more unbearable.

She laughed at herself. Of course Harvey wasn't bad. What nonsense! Just because he drove a hard bargain and knew how to handle staff did not mean he was not good. Maybe he was not sweet. Alright, he definitely was *not* sweet! But he was attentive and correct, and despite his initial gruffness, he was often gentle and kind. And now, at long last, he was very slowly starting to bond with Sydney. They had a lot in common, it seems. At least that's what she thought as she stared at her face in the mirror. But how could you ever know? What do we ever really see except what they want us to see? Everybody is like the façade of a Moorish home – nondescript, secretive, jealously guarding whatever lies beyond the whitewashed walls. Inside there could be fountains and ornate archways, but from the outside you would not be able to do more than venture a guess. Or like the repetitive doors of apartment blocks where the only element of distinction is a change in the number or the doormat. And people look at you through the spyholes in the doors, or open their homes just a little, as far as the chain allows. Even if they invite you in and show you round, you are always no more than a visitor. So how could she possibly claim to know Harvey, or Pet, or even herself for that matter?

She concluded that it was probably best not to dwell on it. A waste of time really. She winked at herself in the mirror; everything was going to work out fine. Time to go and see what the boy was up to and let Pet get on with her chores.

Luz was busy sorting out the bed linen and the bathroom towels in a utility room not far from where Andrea was examining herself inside and out. Had she been able to hear Andrea's thoughts she would have agreed with her. It was so difficult to fathom a human soul. After all her years at the house, how many people could she honestly declare that she knew, knew well? Was she any wiser now about the true characters of Alice or Stein or Sydney than she had been when they had first taken her on, shortly after the master's death? She was pretty sure they knew next to nothing about *her*.

Señora Luz was in reality señorita Luz, but Alice Haute had decided on hiring her that 'señorita' sounded too frivolous, almost insulting. Was she simply unmarried, or a spinster? Was she a young, foolish girl, or a fully trained housemaid? Señora Luz it became. Now Mrs. Haute was in her grave alongside her husband and her son. But what did Luz know of that strange lady? Had she ever understood her? What a mass of contradictions that woman had been. At times the perfect lady, well-bred, aristocratic almost, a woman who could feel comfortable in stately homes and halls of learning. But at others she was more like a pampered Hollywood star, drinking whiskey on the rocks and smoking cheroots in slacks and bra. Refined and disdainful of foul language, except her own. The perfect widow and mother, but whose overnight bag told a different story.

How you made a mental picture of them all, and how they never failed to surprise you.

Then there was Stein, so much like herself. Reserved, diplomatic, cunning, over-cautious. They say he was having an affair with Alice, but he was far too smart for that. He had his own little secrets, his own little ambitions. Or maybe not. There was man who knew how to cover his tracks.

And now we have Harvey Paulson to examine. A man who charms his way in and bullies his way out. Who was going to dare an analysis of the new boss's personality? How she would have liked to be able to sum him up in a phrase. But she knew she was incapable of that, even given more time, more evidence. She had failed with all of them to date, so what chance did she have with smarty pants Harvey? He was far too slippery to catch.

She had noticed a definite shift in the atmosphere of late. It was as if everyone were manoeuvring for position, as in some kind of unstated game of strategy. Harvey conferring with Stein, Harvey trusting Bro, Stein supporting Bro, Harvey and Andrea playing happy families. Now even the unheard of: Harvey playing with Sydney. How they all watched each other, trying to guess one another's moves in advance. Or at least that was the impression she had. But perhaps she was getting it all wrong again, who could tell? We are so expert in deceit when the occasion rises.

She looked out of the window and saw Pet coming back from the kennels. Ambrose would be showing Sydney the dogs again, no doubt with Andrea hovering around nervously, unsure whether to trust him with the boy or not, but dying to get away to her idling.

Ambrose and Pet. She made no attempt at categorising them, it would be unfair. They were simple folk. You could almost see inside their brains and watch the words being made, they were so transparent. Borderline? No, just not very bright. Which made machination impossible. Which in Luz's mind made them free of guilt, so they were not to be judged. They were to be left out of things, like children. They would make foolish mistakes and out of place comments, bungle and stumble through their allotted tasks no doubt, but they would always give what they had without so much as a second thought. They were naturals, meant no harm to anyone, and therefore deserved nothing less than pity and forgiveness. It appeared that Harvey had scented this latent support for them, because he had eased up on Bro ever since that letter. Maybe he had realised he would have to face a rebellion, a mutiny, if he tried to lay any blame at Bro's door, or Pet's come to that. He was a shrewd customer all right.

She would have to keep her wits about her for the time being, until things settled down again, until the new pool was built and the family left for Kenton Beach. Then perhaps they would all have a bit of peace and calm.

Andrea had never liked dogs. Her neighbour had had a
Yorkshire which had been pretty and cute, with a bow in its hair
and a little jacket for winter, but that had been more like a toy
than an animal. And guide dogs were nice in a boring,
responsible way. Apart from that she hated the beasts. It wasn't
so much the sniffing and dribbling, the damp hair smell, the
foul breath, the scratching and licking and genital hunting
habits that so irritated most dog haters. It wasn't their ferocity,
or their warm deposits, or their comical sexual urges either. It
was that they reminded her so much of people. By which she
meant 'other' people.

Other people were all those who existed outside her closed
circuit of friends and family. Other people eked out their days in
submissive servility and unquestioning loyalty. Their lives were
a homogenous routine of stupidity and dependence. They came
in all shapes and sizes but rarely got beyond chasing sticks.
Once she had seen a man on the beach beating his dog. That
huge animal could have jumped up and taken out his throat with
one snap. But it didn't. It got beaten then came back for more.
So much for dumb animals. Luckily for her she was a breed
apart.

The kennels had been tacked on to the back of the garages, a
fenced off area where the three dogs were kept most of the day.
A strip of green construction site cloth supplied a little shade,
and here the dogs would lie and doze, scratch and dream, or lap
at semi clean water from an old saucepan. They were guard
dogs, at least officially. Cross breeds all of them, a curious mix
of Alsatian, Doberman and other bits and bobs of genetically
engineered canines. Mongrels, Sydney had explained to her
with a smile on his face, because the pedigree ones were worth
more than the junk they were defending. Then he told her
another one of the Haute House anecdotes which she was to
inherit on agreeing to marry him. One night there had been a
burglary, but instead of breaking into the house itself, the
thieves had come for the dogs. When the household woke up

the following morning they found that the poor things had disappeared, the whole lot of them, without so much as a yap.

She was relieved to see that Sydney had not been allowed inside the pen, and had to content himself with stroking Dusty's nose through the meshing of the fence. Dusty was to be trusted. He was old now, and enjoyed being made a fuss of. But Digger and Ringo needed to be watched. They were nervous beasts, forever going round and round in circles inside the pen, or twitching and shivering as if they had heard some unsettling noise. They made Andrea feel uneasy just by watching them. Ambrose was inside, cleaning up some mess or other, changing the water, whatever it is one does inside a kennel compound. The dogs followed him about as if they expected something from him, some kind of treat, a titbit maybe, or perhaps he was going to let them out? He'd better not.

'Come away from there, he might bite you.'

Ambrose looked up. He wanted to say that Dusty was safe enough, that he enjoyed the attention, that it was good for Sydney to get to know the dogs, it was much safer that way. But that was not his place, as he well knew. So he just kept on sweeping.

Sydney didn't move. He never did what his mother told him, at least not at first. They had established that many moons ago, it was their natural relationship.

'Sydney. Come on. Be careful.'

Nothing. She contemplated him for a few seconds, unsure whether to snatch him away by the arm and drag him back to the house, or to storm off and leave the little brat to it. Her protective fear won the day.

'Come on, you can play with Dusty later if you are a good boy. If you come now you can take him for a walk in the grounds this afternoon. Is that o.k., Bro?'

Ambrose nodded. Yes, yes, of course.

'But you have to come now. Stop stroking him and come back into the house. We have to wash your hands now after touching the dog. Come on, you haven't even brushed your hair yet.'

Sydney looked at his mother suspiciously.

'I promise. This afternoon. Ask Bro. That's a promise, isn't it Ambrose?'

'If that's what you want. Yes.'

'You see. So come on, let's get ready for when Harvey gets back'.

She took his hand and led him back to the house.

Ambrose finished his tasks and sat down in a corner of the pen. The dogs came to him and lay at his feet. He also thought that dogs were like people. They liked to be loved, they often felt lonely, or bored, or sad. They were loyal to each other and to their masters, noble and intelligent, and would give their lives for the ones they love. Like the rest of us they had feelings. Ambrose adored them, and the feeling was mutual.

'I promised he could take Dusty for a walk this afternoon.'

Stated tentatively. She did not want to give the impression that, in her opinion, Harvey ought to take his step son through the grounds. Neither did she want him to feel that she was fobbing the boy off on him so that she could be alone. She was simply tossing out an idea, and he could either catch it or let it drop. Whatever. Naturally she hoped that her tolerant, non-committal tone would work, that he would feel obliged to follow her cue and offer to take Sydney for a walk of his own accord. She could see no reason why he should refuse, but....

Harvey was used to these ploys by now and paid no attention whatsoever. He had his own agenda, which may or may not coincide with that of his wife. As it so happened, being with Sydney, being seen to be with Sydney, was now a priority. A walk though the grounds with Dusty. Perfect.

'Fine. Once I've got off those papers, say six o'clock. We'll give the old dog a run for his money.'

Andrea smiled. It had been a long time coming, but at last a semblance of a family could be discerned.

'I'll go and tell him, he'll be thrilled.'

At the kennels Harvey ordered Ambrose to fetch Dusty. He was comfortable in the old dog's company, but did not trust Digger's or Ringo's intentions. On more than one occasion he had tried to assert his authority over them, but they had always kept their distance and snarled menacingly at him. He did not like them; they were too autistic, too ferocious. But then that was their allotted task; they were not family dogs but guard dogs. Ambrose brought Dusty out on a short lead and handed him over to Harvey.

'Here, you take him. Hold him firmly, like this, a little nearer, that's it, and with the other hand... That's good. And remember that he needs to know who's boss, so you are in command, o.k.? Let him know that. He is the dog, you are the master. Once he sees that everything will be fine.'

Harvey was unable to contain his desire to control the situation. He had explained all of this to Sydney, to Andrea, even to Bro, a hundred times. It was so basic that it went without saying. But Harvey could not restrain himself; he would give a lesson in dog handling whether you wanted it or not. And it was better to listen and suffer in silence, or he would find an excuse to fly into a rage. Then there would be no walking the dog, no talking, nothing, until he had calmed down again. So Sydney, overjoyed at being able to take Dusty out on his own, albeit with his step-father in tow, decided that prudence was the best councillor.

To prove his point about showing the dogs who was their master, he kicked the wire meshing and growled at the two remaining dogs. They began to bark furiously, threatening to leap at the fence in an attempt to attack Harvey.

'Down! Down I say!'

The dogs continued to bark and show their teeth, livid with anger. Dusty began to pull at his lead.

'Hold him tight. Show him who's boss. Down, down with you!'

He turned away suddenly, with an arrogant gesture, the bullfighter's disdain for the humiliated beast, and led Sydney off towards the gardens. Behind him Digger and Ringo continued to snarl and bark, pacing the compound like rioting prisoners. Now Ambrose would have to spend time with them, soothing them and talking to them until they realised there was nothing to fear.

Pet, who had been smoking by the side of the garages, strolled past the kennels with a nonchalant air.

'Well, that showed them who's the boss, eh?'

Then broke into a half cough half laugh. Ambrose started to laugh too. What a fool that Harvey was at times. What an idiot.

Once in the grounds Harvey could ignore the boy. Dusty was let off the lead and allowed to roam, while little Sydney tried unsuccessfully to gain Harvey's attention. He fired questions at him at high speed, but soon realised there was not going to be an answer. So he ran after Dusty, keeping up a narrative of his own, every so often calling out to his step father, who stoically refused to be drawn in. Surely he had done enough by offering to walk the grounds with the lad without having to feign interest in his childish banter? He had been seen, the effort had been made and noted, that would have to do.

'Look, Harvey, look!'

The boy was pointing at something with a stick.

'What is it, Harvey? What's that?'

Sydney did not call Harvey 'dad', or 'father'. At first Andrea had suggested that it would be, from a psychological point of view, best for all of them. It would help create the idea of a family, would strengthen the bond between them all. Harvey should perhaps call Sydney 'son'? After all, to all effects Harvey was indeed now the boy's father. It could only help, she argued.

Harvey was horrified at the idea, though he managed to control himself and hide this from Andrea. He knew he would never be able to call the little brat 'son', and to have him running around calling for 'daddy' when his real father was long dead, though unfortunately not forgotten, was too much to demand. Because Harvey did not love the child. Not only did he not love him, he did not even like him, or want to be with him, or have to live with him and educate him for the rest of his life. As far as he was concerned the world would be a better place if little Sydney Haute would just disappear. For good. Wishful thinking? Quite likely, but he thought that only then could he concentrate on building his own family with Andrea. Then he would be in complete control.

But he realised that he would need to argue his position, to carefully edit his words. Andrea must never suspect his true feelings towards the boy. He needed her, and the household too, to believe he was at least willing to make an effort. So he explained his position. He felt that it was not good to falsify reality. Sydney should always know who his father was, and be encouraged to cherish that knowledge. It was part of his heritage, and would eventually become part of his character. Sydney should see Harvey as a caring, father-like figure, but should at all times be aware that the real father, the blood father, was the late Sydney Haute. To use terms such as 'son' or 'father' would only confuse the child. A time would come when he would have to be told the truth, and that could be a dramatic moment if he had been led to believe that Harvey was his father. Adoption agency counsellors recommended the truth from the beginning. It was in the child's best interests. Despite the temptation to play the role of a father, he only wanted what was best for the lad. He would have to insist. Sydney would call him Harvey.

Andrea, unconvinced, checked with the adoption agencies. It was the preferred approach, apparently. So she let it go, for now. There would be time, it was better not to rush things.

Sydney continued to run after Dusty and to fire unanswerable questions at his legal guardian. But Harvey had a lot on his mind. Apart from his everyday work, there was the pool area to think about. Work was coming on, the pool itself had been retiled, and soon they would be filling it to check for possible leaks. The wood had been chosen and ordered, and would arrive any day now. That fool Ambrose had all he needed too, so he would soon set to work on the electrical installation. Little by little Harvey would transform the house into something that reflected his own taste, his own style, his own character. He would make it his, he would leave his mark.

Time for one last tour of the grounds. With any luck Brendan and his son would see them before they finished for the day. The more witnesses the better.

How much of this was an elaborate chess move, how much the spontaneous improvisation of an intelligent man? Ask Harvey today and he will deny it all. Is he being insincere? Is he covering his tracks? Is his attitude Machiavellian? Or does he really believe that events unfolded the way he describes them? Are atrocities part of a well-planned conspiracy, a carefully designed campaign, or are they moments of fumbling stupidity? Is murder a strategy or a fatal mistake? Or perhaps no more than an over-exaggerated survival instinct? Either way the end was clear; he wanted a world without Sydneys. And Harvey was accustomed to getting what he wanted.

There are as many versions of what happened on that fateful day as key players. What Pet saw and heard did not necessarily coincide with what Andrea had witnessed. The unfurling of events according to Mr. Stein did not entirely match what

Señora Luz told the police. Harvey's tale of the trail of incompetence that led to tragedy bore little resemblance to the bewildered yet stubborn declaration of Ambrose. Their statements were like so many gospels, each one narrating the same story, but from varying angles.

'The truth will out', Pet said solemnly, but it was more of a wishful prophecy than a hard edged fact. The truth is chameleonic. Like beauty, it is in the eye of the beholder. So it comes down to which version you prefer to believe, and in this choice social success once again is a determining aspect. A respected and wealthy member of the community is more likely to be believed than those involved in menial tasks. An influential and eloquent person has more shares in the truth than the unskilled labourer. As Harvey well knew.

The workers had cordoned off the pool area with battered metal barriers and red and white plastic tape, much as the police would do later, in order to maintain the safety regulations. It was in the interests of everyone to obey their instructions. Only qualified personnel were to be allowed inside the working zone. Anybody entering the area did so at their own risk. The rules were to be strictly observed or the insurance company would do what it had done to Spotty's mother. That was the theory. But Haute House was private property, the labourers soon got to know the household staff, at the weekends nobody was around to make sure the regulations were followed to the letter, and a certain laxity crept in. Pet often wandered in to see if anybody would like a cup of coffee or tea, especially the balding one with the thick eyebrows who seemed to take an interest in her, even if she realised that he was only really fantasising and had no intention of going any further than that. She enjoyed the flirting. Mr. Stein, as overseer, came and went as he pleased, often accompanied by Andrea or Luz. There were no hats, no protective boots. Just be careful and use your common sense, they were told, that should be enough. Even Sydney sneaked in every now and then to watch the men as they cut tiles or loaded skips with rubble. He loved to climb the sand piles, much to Andrea's horror. Pet watched over him to make sure he came to no harm, and got up to no mischief.

The job was coming on nicely. The whole area had been levelled, and Ambrose was busy laying down the power cables for the lighting. The wooden boards had arrived late on Friday evening while Harvey was still at his office in the city; he would be inspecting them Saturday morning to make sure he had not been duped. Meanwhile a green and yellow hose pipe very slowly, almost imperceptibly, filled the pool.

Saturday morning at Haute House was a dress rehearsal for Sunday morning. Tense, weekday muscles began to relax, clocks lost their rigidity, and movements became less mechanical, more fluid. It was not the total collapse of the system that Sunday demanded, but rather the transition from activity to inactivity. Harvey rarely went into the office at weekends, Sydney had no school, the gardeners were hardly ever to be seen, Andrea had no tennis classes or massages, and usually avoided the shops, always so busy at weekends.

Breakfast was served later, and eaten at a slower pace. Newspapers were read for once instead of being briefly scanned. Obligations remained, especially for the household staff, but there was an air of flexibility about Saturdays and Sundays that made even the most onerous tasks more bearable.

The semi relaxed weekend atmosphere at the House helped explain why, when interrogated by the police, most of them answered vaguely and without precision. They woke up 'around' eight o'clock. They had breakfast until 'nine, nine-thirty'. They had trouble remembering exactly who was with whom, and where. When was virtually impossible. That made the reconstruction of events extremely difficult, and very frustrating. At times they would contradict each other, even themselves, then apologise profusely when this was pointed out to them. The problem with justice, with discerning innocence from guilt, is that we are all such poor witnesses. Which means that the evidence is often weak, or flimsy, or even manipulated. But judgement is passed nonetheless.

Ambrose woke up, as always, at half past seven, but unlike on weekdays he did not actually get out of bed until eight o'clock. He had a lie in. It was a time for half dreams, for body smells, and for other activities he was not proud of but enjoyed immensely. It was his weekend treat this extra half hour in bed, and helped to keep his mind off sex for the rest of the week. Saturday would rid him of the pent up desires of the week, Sunday would drain him enough to make it through to Wednesday or thereabouts when he might be forced to sneak in another one. He knew that Pet knew, well, most of the time, and that she couldn't agree more. It was far better for him to masturbate twice a week than to have him pining and making a fool of himself over some tart or other from the town.

His sister had decided long ago that she would take control of Ambrose's love life. Ever since that bitch Annette had tried to weasel her way in with her sinuous charm and her thin lips, smiling so sweetly as she squeezed him dry. Bitch. 'Can you lend me some more money, can I borrow your sister's earrings, can you run me into the city, can you promise to always bring me a present, can you do anything I ask whenever I ask it if I let you touch my tits?' She was a scheming little whore, that one. She had poor Bro hanging around her like a beaten dog. She would make him wait outside in the rain while she got rid of another man. What a slut. And Bro none the wiser, moping around and thinking that that was love. So one day Pet had it out with her. She waited for her outside the hairdresser's where she worked one windy evening and gave it to her full blast despite the stares of the passersby. Stay away from my brother or I'll slice you open like a fucking water melon. Annette had sneered, tried to hold her ground, had sworn that they were in love. So Pet had punched her hard on her oh so thin lips and told her once more – like a fucking melon. She had not been seen since.

That had been when they were still living in their parents' house. Maybe Annette had hoped for a stake in that. Well she could go and fuck the bailiffs. Since then Pet had encouraged her little brother to buy magazines. It was safer. He'd had quite a stack of them in the rented flat, but they had judged it best not to take them to Haute House just in case he was caught with them. Now he worked from memory.

Every so often, on his trips into town, Ambrose would meet a girl. He was quite good looking, and although he was not the brightest star in the sky, there were still plenty of young women who found him attractive. But Pet soon grounded him if she suspected anything. She would find excuses to keep him on site, and veto any attempt at contact from any female stranger. Bro was hers, and had to be protected. For his own good. Which is why he had no mobile phone, no credit card, no vehicle. And it was Pet who shopped for his clothes and laid them out on the bed for him each morning. Nothing too dowdy, but nothing too upbeat either. It was she who chose his tattoos and where to put them, if he should or should not pierce his ears, how to cut and dye his hair. So, groomed and dressed by his sister, Bro became what Pet preferred a man to be. He was her male doll, and she was proud of him. As long as he didn't make a mess of the sheets.

Downstairs in the kitchen Pet, who like Luz had been up since seven o'clock, had his breakfast ready. The women had already eaten, and Joe Stein wouldn't be in before nine, so Ambrose had the table to himself, which he loved. He sat at Stein's end, presiding the table, and spread one of the newspapers out in front of him, open at the sports page. He would take his time, have two coffees, maybe one slice too many of toast, and dilly dally until just before nine, when he was to set to work again on the lighting.

'I see the planking arrived. They could have left it somewhere else, instead of just dumping it halfway up the path.'

Pet took a long time to warm up in the mornings, and was often grumpy. Later on, after a few cigarettes and cups of coffee she would return to her jovial self. But not first thing in the morning.

'They said they were running late.'

Always so gullible.

'They wanted off for the weekend more like. Now you know who's going to have to lug it all up to the pool, eh?'

Ambrose shrugged. Another job to be done. It didn't make much difference really, there was always something.

Pet insisted.

'The boss man will want to know why they didn't leave it up by the pool. He won't be too happy when he sees it this morning.'

Ambrose thought about that for a moment. His sister was implying that he was in for trouble, but that didn't make sense.

'He must have seen it already, when he came home.'

'No. He came round the front, so he's in for a nasty surprise, which means.....'

She tailed off; they both knew what she meant.

Ambrose read a piece about basketball and key players and finances, but he wasn't taking it in. He was planning out the morning in his head, running back over the installation plans to make sure he hadn't left anything out. He could always hear his father when he had an electrical job to do, reminding him, encouraging him, bawling him out if necessary so that nothing was forgotten, no important detail overlooked. This morning he hoped to be able to do a trial run, stringing the lamps together one by one and testing them as he went. Once the first one was up and running, the rest would be a simple matter of repetition. It was something he was really looking forward to, as he felt sure that once Harvey realised that he was worthy, that he knew exactly what he was doing, then his position at the House would be reinforced. He would, as Joe had promised him, go up in the world.

He pushed his plate away and sighed the way his father had sighed. It was a sigh that said well, much as I would prefer to sit here all day in your wonderful company, I have a job to do, and I'm a responsible man, so I will now take my leave and go and do whatever is to be done to bring home the bacon.

'Don't forget to rinse your things and put them in the dishwasher. I've got enough to do.'

As always, he did as he was told.

Pet was right, Harvey blew his top. Or at least he went through the motions, played to the gallery, and allowed himself to vent his emotions. Because whether he was truly enraged by the sloppy depositing of expensive wares, or whether he just felt that he had grounds enough and therefore exercised his right to be angry, it was difficult to tell. Later, it was even suggested by some that he had feigned it all to cover his tracks, but that was dismissed as idle talk. Either way, the household soon found out that he was not happy.

Harvey Paulson made his appearance. Dressed in navy blue shorts with turn ups, a matching short-sleeved polo neck despite the early morning chill, and a pair of white trainers that looked as if they had just been taken out of the box for the first time. He stopped in his tracks when he saw the delivery. If it had only been the inconsiderate unloading of the wooden slats far from the area where they were to be employed, perhaps Harvey would have been able to contain his irritation. But on further inspection he noticed that some of the boards had lost their plastic protection and had been badly chipped. Intolerable. It was always the same; the moment he turned his back corners were cut, goods were damaged, jobs blundered. So he unleashed the wrath of the just.

Swearing is not what it used to be. Political correction has curbed some of the more traditional expletives, especially those dealing with religions and sexual preferences. But dimwits were still fair game, and did not enjoy the protection afforded to other minority groups.

'What bloody idiot, what type of fucking *clown*, would just, just, *dump* the whole fucking lot right here, right here in the fucking.... what a total bunch of total idiots, right in the middle, look, so no-one can come and go. Where's the fucking pool, eh? Where?'

As an audience he had Ambrose and Joe in the front row, and Luz and Pet in the gods, watching him rant from the safety of an upstairs window.

'And look! Look! Trashed, useless, might as well just throw the money straight into the bin.'

He picked at the plastic shreds on one of the corners of the stack. Ambrose and Joe braced themselves for the next part of the tirade; blame.

Harvey composed himself in an exaggerated fashion. He was a reasonable man, he was going to try to be calm, despite the incompetence he was forced to deal with on a daily basis, and he was going to get to the bottom of this absurd and avoidable situation. Heads would roll, naturally, but they would roll under his supervision. He ran his fingers through his dark hair and inhaled noisily.

'What time did they arrive?'

Mr. Stein was about to answer but had no time, because Harvey continued.

'What time, exactly, did they arrive, and who let them in? Who let them in, and who supervised the unloading? Who allowed them to.... to.... do this, and who signed the forms?'

He knew the answers to most of the questions, but needed his underlings to understand where each personal responsibility lay. Of course Ambrose had let them in, that was his job, especially when Brendan was not around. Stein had signed the forms, that too was his assigned role. So the only important question was who had overseen the actual positioning of the pallets and why had they agreed to that madness. Harvey had his suspicions.

Joe gestured to Bro – leave this to me.

'They arrived late on Friday evening, just before dark, around eight o'clock'

'Around, around....'

Harvey shook his head, but Joe continued.

'Ambrose let them in, and while two of them unloaded I went to the office with their head man to sign the papers. I should have previously checked the goods.'

'If you had you would have noticed that some of them are badly damaged and of no use whatsoever.'

'Yes sir, it was an oversight on my part that I will sort out first thing Monday morning.'

Stein was forgiven, for having come clean, and forgotten. That left Bro.

'You, of course, thought that dumping these, these, faulty goods in the middle of the path at least a hundred metres from the pool area where they are to be deployed was a fantastic idea?'

Silence.

'Well, mister brain dead, did you think, no, wait a minute, of course you don't *think* , do you, that's the problem. What did they say, eh? Let me guess. "we'll just leave them here 'cos we're in a bit of a hurry, ok?" Am I right, Ambrose? And you naturally agree, because you don't fucking *think*! What a moron, what a total fucking blockhead. Where's the pool, stupid, where's the fucking pool? You going to able to find it when you start work on those lights today? It's over there, Mr. Ork, over there!'

Dumb silence.

'Well you can clean up you own fucking mess. Get these, all of them, up to the pool by lunchtime or...or, and out of the way. By lunchtime.'

'Harvey swung round to storm off in style, but Ambrose needed to ask a question.

'Before the lights, or once I've done? I was going to test run them this morning.'

Harvey looked his hireling up and down as if he were some strange creature that had been recently discovered in a remote jungle. It was incredible. You could hurl abuse at him, load him down with chores and menial tasks, and there he was, unruffled, still unsure what to do but always willing to obey. It disarmed him.

'Oh, after the test run then. But I want those shifted by midday!'

This time he managed to storm off properly. He made for the house via the pool area, kicking at things as he went and swearing audibly. He intended to exude fury for most of the morning, convinced that it gained him respect.

It didn't. Pet thought he acted childishly. What was a grown man doing huffing and puffing like that over nothing? The man was a fool. Luz found this type of behaviour intolerable too. It was basically selfishness. He claimed for himself the right to be angry, the right to be rude, the right to insult. He had a lot to learn. Stein saw it as a lack of managerial skills. He had no idea how the boss ran his successful office in the city, but those techniques would never work at Haute House, because shouting down your staff isn't good practice and won't achieve results in the long run, he was sure of that.

The scene upset the normal running of the house. There would be less communication now, less dialogue, less coordination. Certain members of the household would avoid others, and a tacit silence would fall over the place until Harvey showed signs of improvement. Until then they would all be in a kind of mourning, like a rehearsal for the real tragedy which was about to strike, all of them getting on with their respective days in solitary as far as was possible.

It was just before twelve o'clock that Pet realised that she had not seen little Sydney for a while. Technically he should have been with his father, as Andrea had set aside Saturday mornings for her digital contacts, her virtual friends. She would be lying on her stomach on the double bed, her laptop open. Do not disturb. That meant that Harvey would be expected to look after the boy, maybe take him for a ride round the grounds, or a play a game of some sort. It had taken Andrea years to get the two to spend time together, and now she had managed to turn it into a kind of routine. So from eleven to almost lunchtime, Sydney was in Harvey's care. Except that today Mr. Paulson was best not approached. Had anybody thought of that? Nobody had said anything to her, so she assumed that *somebody* was watching out for the boy. Still, best check. She went to look for him.

That is how Pet knew when quizzed by the police that they found the boy's body at twelve o'clock, almost to the minute.

The tragedy struck her like a blow to the guts. One minute she was searching for a naughty boy, the next the whole mad world was shattered into tiny, razor sharp fragments. Sydney was lying face down in half a metre of water. He was wearing dark shorts and a very yellow T-shirt which looked almost surreal in the bright midday sun. His blonde hair floated gently around his head like a halo. A hose pipe dangled indifferently at one end of the pool, and by the metal steps was a grey cable, an electrical cable, one of those that Ambrose was using to install the pool lights.

Her sudden, sharp screams alerted the whole house, and within seconds the pool was surrounded by every member of the household. Stein was the first to react. He yanked the cable out of the pool and jumped in, snatching young Sydney up in his arms. He passed the limp body up to Harvey, who did not seem to know what to do. He accepted it meekly, in a trance, and for a second seemed more concerned about not getting wet than reviving the child.

Advice and commands began to fly. Call an ambulance, give him the kiss of life, pump the water out of him, save him, raise his legs above his head, move aside, give him room, pinch his nose. Words of common sense to make more bearable their hysteria. The boy was obviously dead, but that was not possible, that was not a reality that could be accepted for an instant, so they continued to run about and shout and scream and cry. Andrea fainted at the first sight of her little boy face down in the shallow water and now lay by a small mound of earth; Pet was next to her on her knees, seized by a coughing fit; Luz wrung her hands and moaned continuously; Stein, taking refuge in practicality, had gone inside to call the hospital and the police, while Harvey tried in vain to blow life back into the child, pushing down hard on his chest, rolling him over, lifting his head, brushing the hair off his face and gently slapping his cheeks. To no avail. And Ambrose, stunned into silence and inaction, stood with his mouth open and his hands on his head, swaying from foot to foot, unable to believe that Sydney was dead, like his father, or that he had seen that grey cable, the cable they had all seen, the one Stein had so quickly removed, dangling, hanging by the ladder. His cable. One of the ones he had been testing that very morning. He knew they had all seen it, knew what they were thinking, knew that they thought that he was, at least partially, to blame.

But that was impossible.

Impossible because Ambrose was, if nothing else, methodical to the point of obsession; it was the only way he had of making sure he made no mistakes. He had laid the cables out in parallel, just as his father had taught him. Neatly, side by side, one for each connection. He had counted them several times, and double checked. Then, one by one, he had connected them, tested them, then disconnected them again. Only when each one had been carefully tested would he proceed to the final definitive wiring. It was laborious, and quite probably unnecessary, but it was what his father had shown him to do, and he did not have the initiative to do otherwise.

So how had a live wire managed to roll over into the pool?

The ambulance arrived and took the tiny corpse away. Andrea had to be swiftly sedated before she lost her mind, so it was Harvey who accompanied what was by now a funeral procession to the hospital morgue. The others stood around in various states of disbelief waiting for the police to come. Perhaps the detectives and forensic experts, with their methods and techniques, could help restore a little order, some common sense, could add an element of logic and comprehension.

Because after the death of a child the world made absolutely no sense whatsoever.

6

Gross negligence manslaughter. That was the legal term. But then there was so much jargon, so much archaic language, so many documents and forms, offices, departments, government employees. An interminable parade of photographs, signatures, fingerprints and statements. The judicial labyrinth. Ambrose was assigned a lawyer, Stephen Bryant, a forgetful, slightly dishevelled young man who spoke too fast for Ambrose to understand and always appeared to be in a terrible hurry. He wore narrow glasses, his fair hair was thinning, and he sometimes smelt of tobacco. He came and went. That was just about everything Ambrose could remember.

Harvey too had a lawyer. Rosaline Gerard. The very mention of her soon struck terror into Ambrose's heart. She was an angular woman, slim and taut, with very straight brown hair, brushed into a middle parting, that she looped behind her ears in a tense way that made her look angry. She wore clothes that could best be described as solemn. Her manner was rapacious. It was as if she personally desired only the very worst for this disdainful Mr. Ork. She badgered, she confounded, she threatened. It soon became clear that she would not rest until this child murderer was severely punished, crushed under the full weight of vindictive law. The lacklustre Stephen Bryant stood in awe of her, and caved in at their first encounter. Rosaline Gerard was not to be messed with. So Ambrose's defence quickly became no more than damage control. He would be found guilty, he would be sentenced to prison. All that Bryant could do was minimise the blow.

Had Ambrose enjoyed the financial backing and social influence of Mr. Paulson, he may have stood a chance. Sydney had died, officially, of electrocution, a discharge which led to heart failure, which in turn was what made him fall face down in the shallow water and drown. That was the conclusion reached by the forensic expert, a conclusion that Stephen Bryant never even dreamt of challenging. A more astute lawyer would have pointed out that, contrary to common belief, clean fresh water is not a very good conductor of electrical current, that the amperage was not at a necessarily lethal level, that a live wire coming into contact with water would have blown a fuse or tripped a jump switch somewhere along the line. They would have demanded a new autopsy which categorically showed lesions to the heart tissue. They would have asked for and found alternative electrical experts willing to testify that the possibility of Sydney receiving a shock large enough and sustained enough to make him fall unconscious was little short of impossible. They would have sown the seeds of doubt. They would have cross-examined Harvey and asked him why he had entrusted the job of rewiring to this man if, as he had noted in his warning letter to Ambrose, he already knew that Mr. Ork was not a qualified electrician at all, but rather a self-taught amateur. They would have asked awkward questions about Mr. Paulson's relationship with Sydney, with Ambrose, with the Haute family itself. In short they would have thrown a veil of uncertainty over the whole affair and petitioned for a verdict of accidental death.

But Bro's representative Mr. Bryant was a busy, underpaid, legal aid defence lawyer with low self esteem and his mind on a thousand other cases, most of them mundane. He visited Ambrose and kept him up to date, but at no moment tried to put a stick in the wheels the judicial process. He filled in the forms, kept the appointments, and informed his client. He knew his place when confronted by Rosaline and her penetrating gaze, and bowed obediently before the reality of the situation – Ms Gerard represented the winners.

During the proceedings Ambrose was held in custody. Not because he was considered a danger to society, or likely to flee the country, or because he could not raise the money for his bail conditions. It was more of a courtesy measure because Bro had nowhere to go. After the incident Haute house fell to pieces. Nobody in their right mind could just carry on as if nothing had happened. The whole place smelt of tragedy. It was as if it had been cursed. The original family had been completely destroyed, Arnold and Alice Haute dead, and the two Sydneys, heirs to a fortune, wiped off the face of the earth by tragedy. The old regime was now gone forever, so the rest of the staff decided it was time to pack their bags and start afresh, preferably somewhere far from the haunted house.

Luz had family up north, a sister and some other less close relatives. She had her savings, and some compensation money for the abrupt finalisation of her contract. There was nothing to keep her at Chester Drive now that Alice, Sydney and Sydney Jr. were no longer alive. Naturally her heart went out to poor Andrea, who was fast turning into a younger version of Alice in her final days; pale, thin, drugged into senselessness, in perpetual mourning. There was an air of gloom and decay that hung about the house now and try as she might she could not chase it away. So she took her leave of Joe Stein. They had spent many years together in service, but they had never really hit it off. She shook his hand and wished him the best. Pet hugged her sincerely, but then she would, wouldn't she? A kind soul, but overweight and smelling like an ashtray. They would write to each other they falsely promised. Taking her leave of Andrea was just like going through the motions, which was a shame because she had truly come to appreciate and feel for her. But the new lady of the house was absent. They too parted on a handshake.

Harvey handed her the cheque and all other relative papers. She knew he was glad to see the back of her, of all the staff. They were the last remaining relics of the original Hautes, the final obstacle. Now the Paulsons could reign in peace. Good riddance, he seemed to say. Same to you, she hoped she managed to get across.

Pet was allowed to stay until she could find alternative accommodation, which she eventually found by shacking up with one of her boyfriends in town. As soon as she had all her belongings ready she was paid and sent packing. No farewells to Andrea, no more than a parting nod to Stein, not a word to Harvey. She was gone. Forget me, she seemed to say. So they did.

Joe Stein 'retired'. He would no longer need to work as his pension was negotiated and guaranteed. Maybe he had the suspicion that he was being bought off, that Harvey was deliberately being over-generous for some Machiavellian reason or other, but he didn't care. He was tired of it all and had no desire to set himself up as judge of any man. He would simply retire, slip off back to where he came from and read, or fish, or watch porn. Whatever, but somewhere they would not come looking for him again with talk of intrigue and death. He'd had enough for one lifetime.

Because there had been so much mutual suspicion going on ever since the police turned up and started asking questions, questions that were not always easy to answer. For a tragedy to take place a chain of events is required, and anyone who has a part in that sad tale, no matter how small, is open to accusation. Everybody had a theory, and once the blamemongery began no-one would escape responsibility, not even the dead. On piecing together the evidence and statements obtained by the detectives, it appeared that Sydney's death was no more than the logical conclusion of involuntary actions, the result of an accumulation of errors. It was as unavoidable as the passing of time.

When we are stripped of social obligations, when we are asked to air the dirty washing of our colleagues, when we are encouraged to abandon allegiances and betray others' trust, then we are all uncannily alike. Almost with relief we confess our worst suspicions. The Haute household was no exception. From

Brendan to Andrea, from Harvey to Petunia, the shit began to fly. If everything that was said was to be believed then they were all guilty to some degree in bringing about Sydney's demise. Posthumous blame was also laid at the foot of Arnold and Alicia's tomb, and not even the supposedly revered Sydney Sr. managed to come out unscathed.

Which worked in Harvey's interests, as Rosaline pointed out. Most of the accusations were hearsay, rumours without fundament, and could be put down to the typical infighting common to closed societies. That the long dead grandparents could in some way be held responsible for the tragic outcome only helped underline the absurd nature of the staff's statements. Apparently they should have educated Sydney Sr. better, should never have let him drive around like a mad thing in those open top sports cars without so much as a safety belt.... Maybe then he would have been around when he was most needed, maybe then that Harvey chap would never have set his clumsy foot in the grounds. And Stein? If he had not walked off with the head man, if he had done his job and overseen the placing of the wooden slats, then Harvey would not have flown into a rage (blame his parents for that) and he would not have lost sight of little Sydney due to his rage. And shouldn't Pet have been on the lookout for the boy? Fair enough, it was she who eventually went to search for him, but why did she take so long? Slouching? Smoking more like. Sra. Luz, so aloof, so perfect, but where was she? Keeping her nose clean again, washing her hands of it all? She had a way of avoiding trouble, thereby avoiding responsibility. But wasn't she paid to keep an eye on things? In the bedrooms she says. Well she had a perfect view of the pool from there if she had deigned to take a look.

On and on it went. Of course nobody was really implying that Stein or Andrea or the delivery men had had a direct influence on the unfolding of events, no, not that, it's just that they wanted to, you know, for the record, draw as clear a picture as possible, nothing more. Far be it from me.

Mudslinging which took the strain off Harvey and his version of the death sequence. He was left the calm, logical, understated path. Rosaline Gerard refused to take on board any of the others' statements. She would stick to the proven facts and draw her conclusions in an orderly fashion in accordance with the law. Really it was quite simple. For one reason or another the little boy had been left unattended. That was not uncommon in a large household, and certainly was not, under normal circumstances, any cause for alarm. The child was at home, surrounded by adults, and theoretically safe. However, due to the negligence of one of the employees, an employee who was undertaking, on his own insistence, a job for which he had no official qualifications, a live wire was left dangling in the pool. Disaster struck, now it was time to assume responsibility. An unqualified electrician who negligently allows a live wire to fall into a swimming pool with children in the vicinity, which later leads to the tragic death of a young boy, must face the consequences of his actions. Nobody else is to blame here. Gross negligence manslaughter. Damages and a minimum sentence of ten years.

Stephen Bryant only had Ambrose's claim that he was always very careful. Not much to go on. The certified letter of complaint, the official warning sent by Harvey, also worked against his client. He was reoffending. Ambrose pointed out that he had not insisted on doing the job, that he had been assigned the task by Harvey himself. But others had made it clear that Bro loved his work and took pride in it, so it was best not to pursue that line. He would fight against damages seeing that Ambrose was all but insolvent, and ten years was of course an exaggerated amount of time which the judge would no doubt reduce to two or three years at most. How they juggled with figures as if they were selling a house! One year, five years, ten years. Who would drive the hardest bargain? Who would strike the best deal, give or take a year or two?

Ambrose looked on in awe as the whole process unravelled,

unable to really take it in. He supposed that the system knew what it was doing, and that whatever decision they took would be in everybody's best interests. The truth will out his mother had always said, so no doubt it would eventually. Luckily he had the ability to feel comfortable in almost any situation. Being in custody didn't bother him particularly; he was at home in a boarding house, in a staff bedroom, in a cell. He was fine with either work or leisure, alone or in company, and could amuse himself in just about any circumstances. He had no idea what would become of him, or if Pet and all the others were going to be alright, but he assumed they would all stick together and pull each other through.

What bothered him most, what took up most of his day, was that wire. It was a mystery. If he had lined all of them up side by side so neatly and carefully.... He went over and over that again. Had he slipped up, had he *thought* he had been meticulous but in reality been sloppy? Was it possible that he had a hole in his memory? Did that happen? Could things that had happened just disappear as if they had never really existed? He had no idea; he was not an expert. But try as he might he could only remember having been extremely cautious and methodical, as he always was when dealing with electricity. He could do nothing else, as he had only ever learnt to do it that way. Perhaps live wires could jump when full of electricity. Maybe a gust of wind. An animal. Over and over again he saw Joe whip the cable out of the pool, the swift glances of Pet and Luz and Sydney's parents. The poor kid face down with his halo of fair hair. Ambrose was unsure what had happened or how, but one thing was certain – he felt guilty.

Guilty not only in a general manner, like not being in the right place at the right time or being unable to do anything to help the boy, but in a particular way too. If he hadn't decided to alternate between cabling and fetching those damned wooden boards. He was carrying a bundle of them when he heard Pet's screams. If he hadn't felt sorry for the delivery men in the first place. They had told him that their boss would dock them wages if they arrived back at depot late, especially on a Friday, and he had wanted to help them out. Some said that Joe should have been in charge, but that was not fair, because someone had to do the paperwork, check the order and sign the receipts. And it was dark. Anyway, it was really only the boss who had made such a fuss. He also felt bad about not having spotted Sydney slipping into the pool. He had seen him running about in the bushes, but had assumed that someone, Harvey, Pet, Andrea, was looking after him, supervising him from afar, because he was not allowed to roam the place on his own. He had seen him but thought nothing of it. 'You think nothing full stop' Harvey had once bawled at him. Looks as if he was right.

'An avoidable death' someone had said somewhere along the line, probably that Gerard woman, and Ambrose could but agree. If only, if only, if only. But he hadn't, and now Sydney had drowned. The cable mystery was still unsolved as far as he was concerned, but it didn't matter much now, nothing could bring the poor lad back to life. Mr. Bryant said that he would probably not go to prison, though he would be sentenced. Sentenced to what then? To not going to prison? It didn't make much sense, but he supposed they all knew what they were doing. It was fair in a way – he was willing to assume his part of guilt in the tragedy. In fact he was even looking forward to the trial as he would get to see them all again. Apparently they would all have to attend, all of them except Andrea, who would be excused on medical grounds. They could catch up with the gossip, and maybe even be able to sort it all out. Joe Stein was a bright man, so he might come up with something. And Luz, with her amazing memory. Pet was shrewd in her own way too and knew how to read signs that most people overlooked. Brendan wouldn't be much help as he wasn't even there. So why did he have to go? Odd. That left Harvey, the boss, Mr. Paulson himself. Surely he could throw some light on what had happened? Yes, it would be a great day. He imagined the courtroom, the high-seated judge, the incisive lawyers, the forensic experts and their fantastic methods to glean the truth from a drop of blood or a thread of fabric. He imagined a jury of earnest, sincere men and women from all walks of life. He imagined a verdict – guilty but not guilty according to Stephen Bryant. Justice would be done, just as his mother liked to say.

Wednesday the seventeenth, ten thirty, courtroom six, first floor. Best suit and tie, hair slicked down, no silly gadgets, no fidgeting, no speaking unless spoken to. Manners at all times.

Once through the security scan the building was impressive, at least on the ground floor. There were portraits of great men, high ceilings, and a double staircase that lead to the upper floors. Everybody wore their finest clothes as if attending a funeral, and some even had gowns like teachers in the old days. They took the left hand flight to the first floor. A wide corridor awaited them. There were his old colleagues, each one forming a tiny group of their own. They came forward one by one and shook his hand, wished him the best, grimaced, then backed away, relieved that that part was over. Ambrose didn't pick up on the negative aspects and greeted each one enthusiastically as if they truly were long lost friends. The police escort suggested he sit down on one of the wooden benches. They waited.

'This won't take too long',

encouraged Bryant.

Ambrose thought he meant the wait.

Forty-five minutes later the case was ready to be dealt with. Stand up, follow me, sit there, now stand up, now sit down again. The trial began.

Bryant was right. There was a crisp parade of witnesses who basically had to ratify their earlier statements. Then Ambrose was made to stand and say 'I swear'. He had to answer some questions about being an electrician and if he could categorically state, beyond all doubt, that he was not responsible for the loose wire being in the pool. He stammered at that point, and there was a generalised sigh. Rosaline Gerard then went into a long and wordy speech which Ambrose found difficult to follow but which appeared to have been very well taken by the presiding judge and by Harvey. Then Stephen Bryant read a brief text which seemed to say basically that it was all a terrible accident and that no-one was really to blame. After that, they had to stand up again before milling back out into the corridor. Ambrose hoped that now he would get a chance to have a chat with his old colleagues, but they all disappeared down the stairs in a flash leaving him to wait for the guard to take him back to the police van. Bryant shook his hand and said he would be in touch.

'But what did he say? Have I been sentenced yet? I didn't hear anything...

'No, Mr. Ork, the verdict will not be through for a few days yet. Try not to worry, I will naturally keep you informed, let you know as soon as the sentence is communicated to me.'

Twenty minutes later he was back in custody.

Seven years. Bryant was clearly stunned and mumbled something about appealing the decision, though he never followed that through. He commiserated with Ambrose, and tried to cheer him up by pointing out that seven years was not ten years, and that damages had been waived. And with good behaviour... He would make sure the penitentiary was an open prison as there was no threat involved, no violence, no fear of escape. He oozed incompetence even when dealing the blow, but Ambrose just felt sorry for him. The poor man had lost his case, and that was not something easy to swallow. Ambrose bore him no grudge; he would go meekly.

It was this meek, docile man, convinced of his inherent innocence yet at the same time convinced of his portion of guilt, that so fascinated and infuriated Richard 'Spotty' Dodd.

On paper they looked like they should have a lot in common. Both were in for manslaughter, both had drawn the short straw socially, both of them were without capital in a capitalist designed society. But in practice they were two very different breeds of men. Spotty was a survivor; he would do whatever was necessary to remain alive and kicking, preferably in relative comfort. He had seen that over the centuries humanity had suffered war, famine, plagues and mutually assured destruction. It had not only overcome those obstacles, it had proliferated, and Richard 'Spotty' Dodd had inherited that survival instinct. That did not mean that he would steal food from a hungry child's mouth, though he would have to admit that he might stoop to *persuading* that child to give him half. Unlike Harvey he did not want it all, but he certainly demanded his share. Bro didn't even seem to realise that he was entitled to a share at all.

For a time Spotty watched Ambrose from afar. He saw how the other inmates cajoled him and fooled him into running errands, into lending them his things which he was too reserved to ever claim back, how they made him take the rap for minor breakages or irregularities of all sorts. Ambrose was not alone in being used like this; there were droves of them both inside and out. They had the mentality of dogs before the alpha male, meekly accepting all abuse as if it were part of a natural process. They accepted their lot almost as if they were robots. Do this. Alright. Do that. Ok. Empty heads.

So Spotty looked on, taking mental notes on Ambrose as if he were part of an anthropological study. The man was unquestioning obedience with a smile, the perfect minion, the ideal servant. There appeared to be no limit to his ingenuity and good will. The temptation was too great for most of the other inmates and Bro soon became the general dogsbody, either immune or deaf to insult, always ready to please, always so easily fooled.

Spotty had not received a full education and would be the first to admit that his general knowledge was full of holes, but he was a bright man with an inquisitive mind, and he was determined to make amends. He read extensively if chaotically in prison, and used the limited access to the internet as often as he could. Finding that he tended to get bogged down with long, erudite texts, he developed a love of quotes, of matchbox and crisp packet axioms, and became a notorious name dropper. He liked to push his glasses back up his nose and say, in a learned way even the layman could understand, 'as Nietzsche said', or 'A man who won't die for something is not fit to live, now who said that, eh?' The other inmates laughed at him, called him 'the professor`, or 'smart arse', and sneered at his apparently useless information, though they secretly admired him too and would seek his advice over 'deeper' issues such as religion, family affairs, or sexual orientation.

He had always seen the world as Us and Them, the Haves and the Havenots. But observing Ambrose he began to wonder if there was not a third class, an underclass, the delta and epsilon workers, an exploited layer of slow, dim-witted mortals whose sole purpose was to supply the rest of humanity, the other two rival factions, with loyal manpower. There was a mass of people who did not strive for more, or prey on others, or fight or ask awkward questions. They could be manipulated without fear of them rising up against you, without fear of them ever even realising they were being used. A tool to be employed, a weapon even. It was fascinating. He had to get to the bottom of it and find out what, if anything, made the likes of Ambrose Ork tick.

So one day he stopped him in his tracks.

'Spotty. Richard 'Spotty' Dodd. Manslaughter.'

He held out his hand which Ambrose took eagerly. Spotty urged him to respond.

'Oh, yes, Ambrose, Ambrose Ork. Negligent manslaughter. They call me Bro usually, though.'

'Pleased to make your acquaintance, Mr. Ork. Bro!'

Now Spotty had his laboratory rat the experiments could begin. First, the specimen's IQ had to be established. That took about two minutes. Under par was the result. The next step was to discover exactly what had happened to Mr. Ork to lead him to his present predicament. Ambrose said he didn't understand the question. Spotty could not resist the temptation to bedazzle his patient with hard learnt terminology, and for a while kept Bro in total confusion by bombarding him with words he knew Ambrose had never used in his life. Very often they made no sense anyway, that was not the idea. It was just a perverse game that Spotty liked to play, harmless fun that helped him maintain his superior status.

'Analogous as it may doubtless appear to the anterior, the encroachment of tragicomedy on your destiny would you say was casual or causal?'

How he loved the look on Bro's face! Any of the others would have realised he was taking the piss and told him to fuck off. But Bro just looked perplexed and apologetic.

'Sorry?'

'Conspiracy theories abound, inferred or otherwise, yet surely the bat of a butterfly's wings...?'

Bro smiled, then looked down at his shoes. He was out of his depth, and wondered why this man of wisdom had ever bothered to strike up a conversation with him. There was something about the bald head, the goatee beard, the round glasses that rang a bell but he couldn't put his finger on it. Either way this Mr. Dodd was far too clever for him.

Spotty realised he had gone too far.

'All right, I'll spell it out for you. What the fuck happened? Can you tell me that? What the hell is a guy like you doing in here? Did you do it, or did you get screwed?'

That didn't seem to help much either, possibly too many questions too fast. This was going to take some time. Luckily that was something they had plenty of.

Over the next few years Bro told his story as best he could. It was a tale, narrated from the point of view of a worryingly neutral observer with the analytical skill and psychological insight of a child, full of blind spots and glaring contradictions. A tale of innocence and ignorance. He rested blame only at his own door, either unable or unwilling to suggest that a third party might also bear some portion of responsibility for what happened to him. The first time he mentioned the incident at the Golden Nugget and his showdown with Alex Cummings, he gave the impression that he had made a mistake by quitting his job. It had been arrogance and anger on his part. He should have just got on with it, he now realised. Live and learn, he concluded. That drove Spotty into a fury.

'Jesus! Yeah, you should have stayed and cleaned up that bastard's mess. He probably got into big trouble with the bosses 'cos of you over that. You should be ashamed of yourself.'

Ambrose nodded. Irony was not the best approach.

'You're a fool, Bro, a real bona fide fucking idiot. You did the right thing! For once you did it like it's supposed to be done. Stuff your fucking job, and stuff the fucking chickens. Best thing you ever done.'

He looked at Ambrose, whose ears were burning red hot.

'You got to stand up to the bastards or they'll just walk all over you. You did the right thing there. Who told you it was wrong? Your sister? Your mates? The fucking neighbours?'

It was despairing at times all this counselling.

'Remember this, Bro. You did the right thing, you stood up for yourself. If you'd done that more often you wouldn't be here today. Got that?'

Why was he doing this? What need did he have to take a moron like Ambrose Ork under his wing? Ork the dork. What was the point of going back over his history and pointing out the errors? What could be gained by showing the man exactly where and when he had made a mess of his life? Was this altruism? Or was it more like self analysis? Questions he asked himself over and over again.

In the meantime he heard about the Wiggins, good old Jack and Sally and the never-to-be bakery, the traumatic eviction from the family home, the dirty jobs at the docks and about how Bro had wanted to marry a girl called Annette, but she broke his heart by suddenly running off without so much as a goodbye. She just jilted him, just like that. Some things were so difficult to understand. Eventually the tale led them to Haute House. That was when the curse had begun.

'Curse?'

'Yes, Pet's convinced that there is a curse on that place. It has been touched, what does she say, touched by the hand, or the wand, something like that, of doom. I can't remember, something about death anyway.'

Spotty burst into laughter. Some heads turned at the other tables to see what was so funny. He laughed until tears rolled down his cheeks, which made Ambrose laugh too through pure contagiousness. Little by little Spotty composed himself.

'Do you believe that too, Bro? Eh? Incantations, spirits, haunted houses? Poltergeist, extra sensorial phenomena?'

By now Ambrose had learnt to simply ignore the bits he didn't understand.

'I don't know, but there were a lot of deaths, it's true. Sydney, then Mrs. Haute, then..... I leave it to Pet, she's the expert.'

'Clare fucking Voyance. Expert? Expert in what, reading your palm, or your fucking tea leaves? She didn't see that Harvey coming, did she, or those fucking Wiggins come to that? Curse my arse. You're the dumb fucking curse!'

He stormed off, leaving Ambrose with alone with a silly smile on his face. He had these sudden mood changes every so often, and they always took Bro by surprise. In that respect Spotty was much like Harvey, he noticed. How could people be so intelligent one minute, then act like spoilt brats the next?

They made amends later. Spotty realised he had offended Bro by offending his sister. It was fine to rant at Bro, but his sister should be respected, it was only right. Spotty agreed. Sorry. The final blow, the one about Ambrose being the curse, being dumb, was not even considered an insult as Bro was immune to that kind of thing. Anyway, they were friends.

Friendship is a relative term, especially in forced situations like prison, the workplace, the army. Spotty was a popular, worldwise man who spent most of his time in the gym, or smoking with his card playing group, or reading in the library. To him Ambrose was a distraction, a pastime, a point of anthropological interest. It was true that he had developed a certain soft spot for the man, though he suspected that that was not down to true affection but to a sense of pity. He would defend him against abuse, though abuse him himself every so often. He would ignore him for days then demand his immediate presence. He would glean information out of him only to throw it all back into his face in disgust. They were not friends; they were cellmates, fellow inmates, colleagues in calamity.

Ambrose saw it differently. To him Mr. Dodd, good old Spotty, was his best and dearest friend; he was the only man who had taken interest in him and his sad tale. Spotty was as near a genius as any man he had ever met, and that a man of such intellectual power should decide to spend so much time with him was... beyond words. He would be eternally grateful.

Not only that. Spotty had at last opened Ambrose's eyes to the truth. The man had listened, and asked pertinent questions, he had gone over and over it again, studying every minor detail.

Not only the facts, like they did at the trial, but the ins and outs, the looks, the things they said and the things they did. And why they did them. Spotty had laid it all open, had unravelled the mess and shown Bro what had really happened. He had been set up, by Harvey, so that Harvey could get the lion's share while thicko Bro took the rap.

How had he been so blind? But that was not fair, as Spotty pointed out. The better question was, how could Harvey be so fucking evil? What a scheming bastard. What a cunning, conniving, sly, creepy... Little worse than the devil himself. He had as good as murdered Sydney, then, oh so cleverly planted all the right clues so that it looked as if it had been Bro, poor harmless Mr. Ork, who had been responsible for everything. Very smart, very sinister. And so far he had got away with it and was now living it up somewhere whilst they rotted in jail.

Justice had not been done, quite the contrary, and things could not just be left like that. If they did nothing, then nothing would ever change. The world would merely tick over as it always had done, and the cheats would win again. Something had to be done. Spotty pulled Ambrose into his room and ordered him to listen attentively, to look him in the eyes and concentrate. He explained that a journey of ten thousand miles begins with the first step, and after a while and a physical demonstration Ambrose was convinced. He told him about Mao, Mousey Tongue, a cross between Che Guevara and Bhudda, and about the Long March. That confused Bro, as it was intended to do, but the general idea was made. Action, Bro, action. So it was that Ambrose and Spotty planned their revenge. Ambrose would carry it out as it was his vengeance after all. Spotty would map it all out for him. Why? Well, call it revenge once removed.

Harvey was not exactly living it up. Yes, the verdict of manslaughter had meant that the child's inheritance had passed on to Andrea, and therefore to himself. Haute House, and the business empire that had made it possible, was now under his control. But it was a huge, empty, unfriendly place now, costly to run and impractical as a residence for just one couple. Andrea, what remained of the original woman he had married, logically loathed going back, she too said it was cursed. She preferred to hide herself at Kenton Beach, which meant that they spent more and more time apart, as he could not be absent from work for any length of time and had to stay in the city. He had a bachelor flat in town, and only visited the house to make sure it was all still ticking over, that nothing was missing, that the rooms were aired and cleaned, that the cars were polished and started up, the grounds tended to. Haute House was now reserved for ceremonies and balls, inaugurations and presentations. Occasionally it was used as a kind of hotel for important guests and clients. It was undoubtedly the jewel in the crown of his property portfolio, but also a bit of a white elephant.

No matter – life goes on. He had finally gained what he had yearned for and was now master of the whole county. He was the richest and most respected man in the area with a mansion that he could afford to use as little more than an elaborate calling card. His wealth was snowballing and his reputation going from strength to strength.

It was not the time to look back into the past. Regret is for the weak. What's done is done. That is what he wanted to say to Andrea, what he most urgently needed to get across to her. She was but a ghost of her former self, permanently undergoing therapy of one kind or another, surrounded by empty headed society women who thought the best thing for her was to drink gin and flirt with suntanned young men. Give her a boost. They were all full of quasi scientific theories – self harm, self esteem, self this and that. And a pill for each one. How he wished she would snap out of it and go back to being the woman he had first fallen for. But she had been trapped in time like a prehistoric insect in amber. Sydney's death, the whole scene, still floated in the air and refused to go away. For her The End never appeared on the screen.

Still, there was little more he could do about that now. They had been through years of treatment and professional help, to no avail to date, and he was getting used to things being that way. He could not worry about that forever, he was a busy man. Things had turned out that way and no amount of crying or heart wringing could change anything now. She should do what he had done; square up to the truth and come to terms with it. No blame, no punishment, no regrets. Just facts and assimilation. Then she would be able to carry on.

Harvey was aware of the accusations made against him, knew too well that many thought he had been to blame for the tragedy. He had so much to win and so little to lose from Sydney's abrupt departure that rumour was always going to paint him as the villain of the piece. That was legitimate, and only to be expected. People judged you with the evidence they had at hand, then added a few drops of personal opinion, shook it all up with likes and dislikes, and finally reached their lop-sided verdicts. But what others thought was irrelevant. The inquiry had found Mr. Ork to be the sole culprit, the only person responsible according to law. Case closed. Let the gossipers and speculators have their fun, it was of no consequence. Because the only person who knew the truth, the whole truth and nothing but the truth was himself.

He had gone over events in his mind and drawn his own conclusions. Not in a moralistic way, and naturally without the slightest trace of sentimentality. Facts are unavoidable, past events immovable. There was little to be gained by trying to decide whether the decisions made or the steps taken were right or wrong. He was no clergyman, no philosopher. Anyway, in his experience the minute you set yourself up as a paradigm of integrity and decency you simultaneously opened the door to hypocrisy. Finger pointers all of them, and stone throwers if you gave them the chance. He had no truck with self appointed arbiters of virtue. To Harvey the whole idea of guilt was absurd. A person is faced with a choice, at a given moment, in unique circumstances. There is no delaying that election; it must be made on the spot. Once that decision has been made and the course of action defined, another choice will present itself. And so on and so on ad infinitum. It's called living. Some moves will perhaps be seen, in hindsight, as errors. So be it. But there is no time to dwell on such theories. Life goes on in that manner until it doesn't any more. To succeed you need to be fast, faster than the rest. To triumph you need to be the fastest. Moral considerations only slow you down.

He admitted to himself, and only to himself, that he had deliberately created the conditions which would favour his ambitions. He had hunted and captured Andrea not only because she was attractive, which she undoubtedly was to his eyes, but because she held the key to a bright and fabulous future. Had she been just a pretty a face, he may still have married her, that was always possible. But the fact that she was heiress to the Haute fortune most certainly coloured his opinion of her. Frankly he had hounded Ambrose at first because the man was a fool, but later because he realised that a man of such limited capacity was malleable and could be useful, either for cleaning up shit or as a scapegoat if required. People of that nature are like tools to be used by their intellectual superiors. Not because they deserve such treatment, that again would be an inadmissible ethical judgement. No, it was purely a question of nature. Ambrose had to get by as best he could with what he had, and Harvey too. There was nothing to be ashamed of, nothing to ask pardon for. And no hard feelings either. Just facts. And Sydney Junior? He had pretended to befriend that little brat, the spoilt, tantrumming son of his wife's earlier love, because he had suspected that the hearsay would then work in his favour. Not the loving father figure, obviously, but at least no outward signs of enmity. He had not hated the boy, that was too passionate a word. But he had not grown to love him either. His death had been a shock, a terrible and tragic surprise. But once again, the idea of blame, of fault, was hardly of any use now. Events had unfolded, and the only thing that Harvey considered himself 'guilty' of was perhaps giving them a little nudge in the right direction. That letter? Foresight. The renovation of the pool area? Pure coincidence, but very handy.

He had kicked Ambrose's neatly laid out wires when he wasn't looking because he was angry and needed to vent it on something or someone. One of them had dropped into the pool. Was it a live wire? He had no idea. Was it a possible danger? What isn't? Why had he not mentioned this to the police, knowing that it could have saved Ambrose from blame and therefore from prison? It was called taking advantage of circumstances. Anyway, the alternative, a confession of guilt, would not have changed anything. Quite the contrary, it could have been devastating. He had let Sydney roam on his own, out of surveillance, because he had had enough of the little bastard. There were plenty of others to keep an eye on him. Did he think for a minute about the possibility of Sydney wanting to play with the water? Maybe. But that was not his concern. Had he consciously prepared the ground so that the little boy would fall neatly into his trap? Of course not. He was not a beast. Was he to be branded as inhuman, devoid of all sensitivity and feeling simply because he conceived the world as a sequence of events not always under his control? Did that mean he had never loved, or felt the pain of loss; did that make him immune to others' suffering? Did it turn him into a deceitful, scheming, evil person who hardly deserved to live? He thought not. At worst he had inadvertently made the outcome move from possible to probable. But any manoeuvring on his part had been instinctive, not premeditated. He was comfortable with that. He was even more comfortable with the fact that he had been right and that Ambrose had turned out to be the perfect fall guy. Sydney's death was a tragedy, and he could still feel his limp, wet body in his arms, still hear Pet's screams, still see his wife slumped on the ground as if she had been struck by lightning. But life was full of nasty surprises and cruel twists. To survive strength was required, even more so in times of crisis. Collapsing in tears was understandable for a time, but in the long run solved nothing, changed nothing. Sydney's turn had come; it was as simple as that. Perhaps Harvey had been part of his rueful demise. So be it. But that was now behind him, and he had other urgent matters to attend to.

7

The guns were kept in a glass fronted cabinet in a small lobby just off the billiard room. Joe Stein had told him that the cabinet was worth a fortune in itself as it was made of walnut or mahogany or something like that, and weighed a ton. Ambrose had often asked himself how one wood could be more expensive than another. Did they do it by weight? Or because it took them longer to cut down? Either way it was beautifully crafted, with lion-like feet and whorls and fluting wherever you looked. Inside the firearms were carefully laid out as if in a museum showcase. You almost expected to see a small label next to each piece with a little information and a date. There were a number of exquisitely decorated antiques, with brass or mother of pearl inlay, and though Ambrose had believed Mrs. Haute when she had told him that they had been used in real warfare by family ancestors, the truth was that they had been acquired over the years as an investment. There were also hunting guns, dull and serious, shotguns that Brendan and his son would sometimes carry v-shaped over their arms, more for show than anything else, as hunting was not allowed at Langley. There was a revolver, too, like Bro had seen so often in detective films, and a tiny ladies' hand gun. But the one Ambrose wanted was the pick of the lot. Harvey's special. It was an exceptionally long-barreled shot gun, standing almost as tall as Petunia. Harvey had told Ambrose he had killed an elephant with that gun, and Ambrose had swallowed that too, of course. And a rhinoceros, a white one.

Harvey's shotgun, Harvey's hunting gun. Except that he had never fired it in his life. It had been a present from one of his better clients, the reverence-demanding, stony-faced Greyson, given to him at the end of his first and last hunting expedition, a two day marathon that he had managed to complete without losing face. Because Harvey was not a hunting man, he found it all just a little too primitive, too close to his animal ancestry for his liking. He preferred to think that he was one step beyond the hunter-gatherer theory, and did not enjoy being reminded of his species' unsophisticated origins. Still, if the signing of a lucrative contract depended on his humouring a cherished customer, well that was part of his job and it would have to be done. So he feigned interest, counterbalancing it with admitted ignorance and apologetic incompetence, and got the damned papers stamped and delivered. Greyson had then presented him with this absurdly long shotgun. Harvey was unsure whether it was meant as a sincere gesture, a kind of 'thank you for being a worse hunter than I', or if it was a cruel joke along the lines of 'see if you can miss with this!' Apparently it was quite valuable, so in the cabinet it went, at the far end on the right, where if just about entered if placed diagonally.

Ambrose knew where the cabinet keys were kept. They were hanging on the back of the cabinet, about a foot up from the light switch, almost out of reach, but if he could just catch hold of the wire with his finger….Of course he could just smash the glass, it didn't matter much now, but he was unable to destroy something so precious when there was no need. That would be vandalism. He unlocked the right hand door and gently eased out the weapon. Spotty had warned him – use your gloves, Bro, touch nothing, wipe it all down. If the forensics get a whiff of you they'll have you back inside in a tick. They can fucking smell you. Forensic frenzy, right? Gloves, wipe, o.k.? Lately Ambrose wasn't as obedient as he used to be, and anyway, he had his own ideas about how this should all work out. He held it in his bare hands. It was beautiful, sleek and powerful, and heavier than he had remembered. The mechanism was smooth but required strength. Ambrose practiced with the shotgun for a while, snapping it open and shut a number of times and lifting it up to shoulder height until it felt comfortable and natural, before loading it with the ammunition which was kept in the lower drawers of the arms cupboard. He caught his reflection in the glass door and liked what he saw. A man of action, prepared to do what only he could do. Now he was ready.

How Spotty loved that idea – killed with his own gun. As soon as Bro had informed him about the guns he knew that it had to be that way. It was poetic justice, he said. He then went on to explain to Ambrose that there were two types of justice. Normal, everyday, human justice, the one that had put them away for so long and that revolved around money and influence and corruption. It had nothing to do with truth or retribution and was much more prone to punishment and revenge. They called it justice because somebody had coined the phrase, but it was in reality no more than a complicated system designed to keep the rich and well-connected from losing the lifestyle to which they had become accustomed. The other one was called poetic justice, which meant true justice he supposed, and existed almost exclusively in books and films, old tales and people's imagination. Though maybe some cynics were in for a surprise today, because Harvey would meet his maker not only via his intended victim but, irony of ironies, via his own fucking long-barreled shotgun! It was perfect. Ambrose didn't follow his reasoning, he couldn't grasp why there should be two justices, and what poetry, which to him meant rhymes, had to do with anything. But by now that didn't bother him very much. He was learning to think for himself.

It was all going according to plan. He reckoned he had about half an hour at least before Harvey turned up, probably more like an hour. He took a deep breath, examined himself once more in the glass, and headed back towards the garages.

It had taken Spotty years to train Ambrose, to convince him, to overcome his reticence and doubts, to get into that thick skull of his not only the plan and all the minor details, but also, and this had been the hardest part, the reasons, the wheres and the whyfores, the underlying philosophy. He had soon realized that

Ambrose did not so much as question what had happened to him. It was as if life was a film, and Bro was just sitting back in his seat with a coke and some popcorn watching it, his mouth half open, unable even to follow the plot yet alone understand it, or glean anything from it. So Spotty had had to prise it out of him, syllable by syllable, putting it all together until he had a clear idea of what had really taken place. That was how he learnt about Harvey and his scheming ways, how he had used poor Ambrose as a pawn in his game of self-important chess, how he had set it all up so perfectly. He was a cunning bastard, that Paulson, but he would not get away with it so easily, not if Spotty could help it.

Eventually, after hours and hours of painful explanation, he had managed to get Ambrose to see that he had been duped. To 'see', not to just say 'o.k., I suppose you're right Spotty', but to actually believe the evidence, to understand it. Slowly, very slowly, it dawned on Ork the Dork that yes, he had been taken for a ride, blamed for something he had not done. Used, a scapegoat, the fall guy, toilet paper, call it what you will.

But that was just the first phase. Now that the fool realised he was exactly that, a fool, he now had to be turned, transformed from a passive, unobservant dimwit into the master of his own destiny. No simple task. But time was on their side.

Now then, Bro, if you have been mistreated, and the one that did that to you has got away with it and is now living the life while you rot away in here....? Gradually nudging the knucklehead in the right direction, planting ideas and watering them over the months, nursing and nurturing, eh, Bro? Talk of justice, of sweet revenge, of impunity and comeuppance, of inherent evil and social injustice, hours of talk, of persuasion, of education, in the common room, in the patio, in half whispers in the library, until at last the numbskull saw the light. Something had to be done, reparation, retribution, and it had to be done by Bro himself.

That was the most tortuous part. It was a path strewn with half understood morals picked up as a child, a vague fear of eternal damnation, the typical but deep-rooted qualms of a decent person faced with a terrible decision, an ugly truth. What a challenge! It was difficult enough under normal circumstances to make someone see that they must do their own dirty work or be crushed in the process, but Ambrose, Ambrose Ork. Daunting. Still it had to be done. Spotty had killed McCormack, but the insurance company had carried on as if nothing had happened. They were still screwing the poor, regardless, trading suffering for profits. Scavengers. Once more the mighty, the bright sparks, the powerful and wealthy, had got off scot free. Like Harvey. Only here was a way for Spotty to do justice, to strike back, to take at least one of them down.

Ambrose was a slow learner, excruciatingly so, but he got there in the end. Now he knew who his target was and why. The next step was the plan itself, the carefully constructed one he was at that very moment carrying out to the letter. As long as he stuck to what they had agreed on everything would work out just fine.

Was Spotty using Bro for his own revenge? Yes, in a way he supposed he was, but that was secondary. The main thing was to get Ambrose Ork to stand up for himself and cut down his oppressor. It was dangerous, admittedly, as Ork could blow it all so easily. Then maybe, though it was not very likely because Bro was to be trusted, of that he was certain, but there was a slight chance that a trail would lead back to Richard Dodd. Oh well, he could take care of himself. At the very least take the credit for having come up with the plan and trained someone like Ambrose to carry it out. Ah, nonsense, Bro would be fine; he had that damned plan burnt into his memory cells like a tattoo.

Ambrose headed back towards the garages. He had to get the electricity back on before Harvey arrived. The alarm had to be working again, and the automatic gates needed to be switched on or Harvey would smell a rat. Everything had to be running as normal with no surprises, nothing out of the ordinary, nothing that could raise suspicion. He worked his way back through the house to the forced kitchen door and walked out into the sunlight. One last cigarette. He propped the gun up against the kitchen wall and lit up.

The final phase was approaching, and he was starting to get a little nervous. It had seemed quite straightforward in theory, maybe a bit tricky to learn, what with all those sequences and warnings and minor details that Spotty had drummed into him. But that was really just memory. Once you had it, you had it, and it was just like wiring. Step one, step two, bit by bit till you reach the end. He had finally learnt his lesson and got Spotty's approval. And now here he was, half an hour away from revenge.

His hand shook as he drew deeply on his cigarette, like a blindfolded man before a firing squad. He was not usually prone to nervousness; his emotions, like his thoughts, ran slowly, as thick as syrup. Alright, he could sometimes snap if someone took his things without permission, or if he saw someone beating a dog, but they were unusual circumstances. He was definitely not a hothead, or a violent man, not at all. Quite the opposite; he saw himself rather as an emotional tortoise, mostly because he took so long to realize what was really going on. He remembered that his first feeling on hearing that mother had died was one of perplexity. What did they mean? That she wouldn't be coming back? That was impossible, because his mother would always come back. She loved them, she had said so repeatedly all his life. Why would she *not* come back? His father's death puzzled him in the same way. What happened to them to make them go away forever? It all seemed so mysterious. It was only later, watching Pet cry day in day out, that his underlying emotions began to surface.

He knew that behind the garages there was an empty, half-finished pool. He knew that Sydney had died there, that a lot of things had changed forever there that day, but he would not be going back to that scene; he would give the whole area a wide berth. He had hoped that if he kept well away, always skirting the zone, keeping his back to it and his eyes averted, that maybe he would not disturb the demons of memory. It didn't work. As he smoked he recalled his shock, his bewilderment, how he had swayed from foot to foot like an idiot, unable to say or do anything, or even feel anything other than a kind of dumb stupor. The hosepipe, the cable, Joe Stein's brief, accusing glance. And Harvey, clutching the poor child to his chest. Could he have feigned that? No, not that part, he was not that cold, surely? It was the aftermath he had decided to change, by lying and scheming, laying the blame at somebody else's door. Pet wailing, Andrea collapsed by the side of the pool. What a scene!

He shook his head as he felt the tears well up inside him. Now was not the time, not the time. He had work to do, and quick, before that bastard turned up with his flashy clothes and his smooth talk. He would turn his sadness into anger and be done with it once and for all. He stamped out the cigarette in a fury, snatched up the firearm and marched back to the fuse boxes.

Harvey was making good time. If he were honest he would admit that he had hurried his lunch and was pushing a little harder than usual through the traffic so that he could arrive ahead of his original schedule. He knew the reason for this haste – Haute House. It was true that he no longer lived there on a permanent basis, and that it was undeniably in need of a refurbishing and a paint job. He also had to agree that it was expensive to run, unwieldy and a bit of a stone around his neck in many respects. But it was his. The whole magnificent estate now belonged to Mr. and Mrs. Paulson. He never tired of entering those imposing gates, of leaping up the steps to the porch and its grand entrance. Those marvelously carved stairs, those beautiful rooms with huge windows looking out on to the immaculate grounds. There was a light, a unique, diffused light that he adored, and an air of grandeur, of history, and of success that still thrilled him. He would be early, not significantly so, but he should be able to clip twenty minutes or so off his eta. Time enough to get those beauties out on the forecourt and really warmed up, dust them off a bit, place them in a kind of semi-circle so that they would take the movie boys' breath away when they saw them crouching in the evening sun like beasts about to pounce.

His driving became a touch more aggressive as he neared Langley. Not far to go now, the last stretch of Ocean Way and then he was back, back home at Chester Drive and the wrought iron HH. The only negative note was that he always had to visit alone; Andrea would not even hear mention of the place. Understandably. To her the mansion was like a mythical mermaid that lured you to the rocks with its crystal clear voice only to drag you down into the depths of the murky waters of death. Haute House was her perdition. She had lost her husband there, then Alice, and finally... Little wonder she refused to go back. At first he had insisted, had thought that it would be excellent therapy for her, face the ghosts and the like, but Andrea was not strong enough for such treatment, and now he left her to it. Right now she would probably be showing off her still remarkable figure on the terrace of some chic bar, or lying on a sun bed with her friends who would talk about the things that truly mattered to them: themselves and gossip. Well, as long as she was happy. In a way it suited him because it strengthened his opinion about the house; it was his, and his alone.

He swung around the last corner and approached the main gates. The whole street was bathed in a dappled and subtly tinted light that filtered through the summer leaves of ancient trees. The word venerable came to mind. Pulling up outside the main drive he took a deep breath. Here he was at last. Home. Then he reached for the remote which was in the glove compartment.

Ambrose checked his list of things to do one more time. He had the lights back on, which meant that the gates would swing open, and that the burglar alarm would now be back on. Now if Harvey entered the house he would have to quickly run to the alarm unit and switch it off before he had the whole neighbourhood calling the police. And if he threw a switch, no problem- lights! He had the gun, and it was loaded. He was in position and ready to act. All he needed now was for Harvey to show up.

With nothing better to do he went over Spotty's instructions while he waited. He was to wait until Harvey came round to the garages. He was bound to do that eventually because that's what he was there for, to get the cars ready. His man had phoned and set up the meeting, and Harvey had agreed, thinking he was in for some easy cash. He would go straight to the garages. If not, then he would do it once he had had a look round, but he was sure to go to get the cars in the end. That's where Bro came in. He would march Harvey inside the garages and close the doors; that would help muffle the sound of the shots. Once inside, he had to get Harvey to sit in one of the cars. Not an open topped one, but a normal one, something he could close the door on and leave the body inside. That would minimize the blood and the noise. It was tidy. Contingency? Just kill the bastard anyway, anywhere. If he didn't turn up at the garages, search him out and shoot him on the spot. No chit chat, just blast him away. Leave the weapon by the body. Wipe it! Then take Harvey's car, it was bound to be worth a lot of money. He had to drive out of Langley and follow the back roads to an address that he had memorized. It was a clandestine garage. Here they would take care of the car, strip it down and paint it, new plates. There was a market for top range models, though not for the vintage cars that Harvey so loved; they were unique pieces and would be impossible to sell. But the a sports car or a four wheel drive was another matter. So he was to hand it over to a man called Bud, and he would get two thousand for it. This was the part of the plan that Bro didn't like. Spotty always got very hazy when he mentioned Bud and the gang, he didn't trust them and inch, that much was clear. Spotty warned

Bro not to cause any fuss or haggle or be pushy in any way. These boys were mean types and if they refused to pay it was best not to insist. At least they would be getting rid of some vital evidence, so they were doing him a favour either way. So just leave the car anyway and get out of there. And disappear.

Ambrose didn't have the nerve or the heart to tell Spotty that he couldn't drive, that he had never been allowed near a vehicle other than to clean it or push it. Also he had no idea how to 'disappear'. What was he supposed to do? Flee to another country? He didn't even have a passport. Or any money come to that. Neither did he have anywhere to go. A murderer can't exactly just turn up at his sister's house and say hi.

He respected Spotty, and recognized his mental brilliance, but there were parts of the plan that he did not agree with, and could not carry out. He would have to keep that to his chest, and he was sorry, but there came a time when he realized, in his own sluggish way, that there were certain things he had to do his own way. Spotty had taught him that, so it was not betrayal or mistrust or anything reproachable. He sincerely thanked Spotty for all his help and guidance. It was just that he needed to think that this time he was not simply following instructions.

The gates swung open and Harvey pulled up at the front of the house. He was torn between two lovers. How he wanted to leap up those steps and enter the grand old house through the main entrance like the returning hero. Walking into that magnificent hall always slightly overawed him, even more so now that he was the sole owner. He would stand at the foot of those incredible stairs and feel the buzz of success and triumph pump through his whole system. It was like a drug, and he wanted his dose, wanted to wallow in it once more. But. Well, there was no-one there to see him, which took a bit of wind out of it, and it would no doubt look a little lackluster after being closed for so long, in need of a dusting and some fresh air. Anyway it could wait. The most urgent matter on his agenda was the cars. He had to get the new garage doors open and drive those motors out on the forecourt before his clients arrived. They often took quite a bit of starting, especially the Lancia, so he'd better not hang about. Once he had them gleaming and in formation the deal should take a matter of minutes. Then he could take a leisurely stroll through the stately rooms of his prize possession.

Had he not been in such a hurry and decided to take a quick look round the house, he would have picked up the scent of a recently smoked cigarette. His senses heightened he may have noticed a meat carver lying on the small two-legged table to his left. He may have seen then that the double doors to the service area had been forced, from the inside. Warily, the trail would have led him to the kitchen area, and the smashed pane, the broken lock. Spotty's plan would now be in need of the contingencies. If he had carried on and searched further he would have discovered that the glass gun cabinet had been raided, and his favourite shotgun stolen. Now on maximum alert he could have taken preventative action. He could have phoned the police on his mobile phone, or made a dash for his car and the main gates. He may even have decided to stand and fight for his hard earned privileges, and gone to the study to fetch his pistol, for he was not without courage.

But Harvey's mind was on how much he could squeeze the movie moguls for, so he eased the car into second and headed towards the garages.

Ambrose heard the sound of tyres on gravel and knew the time had arrived. He clutched the shotgun to his chest and hid up against the side wall of the garages. His heart was beating wildly, and his breath came asthmatically in short gasps. He was to wait until the car stopped. Please wait until the vehicle has come to a complete standstill. He had told Spotty about how he loved to jump off the buses before they came to a halt and Spotty had laughed. But not this time, Bro. You just wait till it stops, o.k.? Wait till he gets out. He may have a gun in the glove compartment, and we don't want to give him any opportunities here, so wait till he gets out and is well away from the car. Then he's yours.

But even the best schemes can often miss out minor details. Bro had to get Harvey inside the garages. That was o.k. because Harvey would have the keys. But what if he refused? What if he just said no, and stood his ground? What then? Or what if Harvey tossed him the keys and said open it yourself. He couldn't exactly pick them up *and* keep the weapon aimed at his rival. So what was he supposed to do? Well Ambrose had gone one step beyond even Spotty's careful planning.

It was a nonchalant, whistling Harvey Paulson that pulled to a halt on the forecourt. He checked his bag for the garage keys, pushed his sunglasses back on top of his head, and fiddled with his phone. Should he call Andrea and tell her he had arrived? That would be the most normal thing in the world to do, surely? Especially as she worried so much about everything and always expected the worst to happen. Give her a quick call. Let her know that disaster had not struck, that he had not been killed or seriously maimed in a terrible traffic pile up, or that the house was still standing and hadn't been burnt to the ground. As far as he could see it had not been occupied by drug dealers or nomads of any kind, either. Just a brief 'all's well' message? The problem was that he would have to mention the name, the place where he had gone and the reason he was not at home now with her. Haute House, Andrea. Maybe it was not such a good idea. She would be happily oblivious of his comings and goings if he simply left her alone. She'd have the girls over, or be flirting with that moron Greg at the beach bar, leading the poor idiot on as she loved to do. Well that was fine, it gave her confidence and was all harmless enough. He'd phone her from town, once the deal was struck and the cars put back. That way he could avoid naming the mansion at all, and focus on gearing her up for his return. He slipped the phone back in his pocket. How was he to know that hundreds of miles away at Kenton Beach Andrea was spiraling down to the cold, sightless depths of depression. Or that they would never see each other again?

Or that her premonitions and worst fears were to be proven right?

He climbed out of the car into the delicious evening light. All around him the garden bloomed in effusive glory and he paused to take in the sight. Bro was wrong; it was not Brendan or Brendan's son who now looked after the gardens. A private company had been hired, and they too did a marvellous job. He breathed deeply, his eyes half closed. It was then that he saw Ambrose emerge from the side of the garages.

If Harvey had had a sense of humour he might have been able to see the comedy in the situation. Unbelievable as it may seem, there was Ambrose, Ambrose Ork, dressed in dungarees as if he were back at work doing some menial chore or other. An enormous, unwieldy shotgun held up at shoulder height pointing straight at Harvey though wavering somewhat. His head slightly tilted to one side, and one eye screwed shut as he tried to aim. Harvey hadn't seen Ambrose since the trial, and quite honestly had not expected or wished to see him again for the rest of his days. The man had been put down, quite rightly, for gross negligence manslaughter, and Harvey had all but forgotten him. And now here he was, pointing that absurd gun at him as if he meant to shoot him.

After the initial shock and surprise came bewilderment. Harvey was genuinely baffled. What on earth could be going on in this man's head to make him take this rash course of action? What did the fool want now? Money probably, they all did. Perhaps this ex convict felt he'd been treated too harshly and wanted some kind of retribution for himself and his fat-arsed sister. Yes, of course, it would be Petunia Ork who was behind all this; Bro was far too short to act on his own behalf. Your money or your life, for heaven's sake. Or maybe he wanted his job back. Wouldn't put it past the cretin. What an oaf. Though most probably there was no thought process behind it at all. He was acting on impulse, like an animal. Ambrose had never had two thoughts to rub together anyway. He was peeved and wanted to show Harvey something, demand something, though Bro himself doubtless had no idea what he really wanted. Still, there he stood, the dumb bastard.

They say that your whole life passes before you when you realise you are about to die. But Harvey did not even contemplate that outcome. What was the point of dwelling on the sordid possibilities of a premature demise? Like those whose lives were a constantly updated version of This is Your Life. He was a man of action, of worldly ambitions, and did not waste time on speculating about death and its possible aftermath. He had no truck with hand-wringers or head-bashers, and could not abide living-room philosophers and idle chat about the hereafter. He knew those who talked about and even planned their own funerals, the music to be played, the photos, all so tear-jerking. They were the self-important and vain set that imagined the pain and suffering their departure would, oh most certainly, cause amongst their loved ones. He found it sickening. Or those that had 'found' god, and now walked around like junkies, high on religion, smirking smugly at the rest of us poor lost souls like the members of an elite club watching the pedestrians file by from the warmth and exclusivity of their private drawing rooms. No, Harvey had never worried about his own death.

Until now. If Ambrose was here now, standing right in front of him, pointing at him with his own shotgun....why had the alarm not sounded? How come the gates had swung open so perfectly yet Ambrose had managed to break in and steal his gun? A shot of fear ran suddenly through his whole being. Something was not right.

Ambrose had a sense of humour, or at least a sense of the ridiculous. He used to love lying on the bed at home giggling with his sister. They would repeat words over and over again until they sounded absurd. Those same words then became like a secret code between them, and if used in the right context could send them into laughing fits which made them cry and sometimes even choke. They also liked to criticize other people, their big noses, their hairy ears, their conversational ticks. So he could have been forgiven for finding the comical side to this moment. In his sights he had Harvey, frozen with fear, dressed in khaki trousers and a pale blue shirt as if he were about to invite you onto his yacht. His chunky adventurer's watch, his slick leather belt with a logo for a buckle, his sunglasses on top of his healthy head of jet black hair. But Bro did not see the funny side, not at all. He was about to kill a man for the first and last time in his life, and it was not a laughing matter. Harvey had helped drown little Sydney, had managed to shift the blame onto Ambrose, and now he was about to pay for that. It was not going to be a comedy sketch.

It was the perfect moment for some famous last words. Ambrose had tried over and over again to imagine this moment, to foresee what Harvey might do or say, and he had tried to prepare a dialogue in his mind which would fit the situation. He wanted Harvey to understand a few things before he died. He needed him to see that Bro now knew everything. How he had manoeuvred so that an accident would take place, how he had so cunningly covered his tracks, how he had perversely prepared the ground so that it was Ambrose who eventually took the rap. He knew how, and he knew why. Firstly because Harvey could, because he had been born a bright spark and rarely missed a trick. But also because Harvey was a climber, a selfish, amoral, over-ambitious man with an insatiable appetite for more. He was unscrupulous and unmerciful. He preyed on his fellow men with the sole idea of personal profit, and fuck the consequences; the rest could go to hell. He imagined how Harvey would try to worm his way out of these accusations, how he would sneer and mock, rant and insult. There would be a string of synonyms – dunce, bonehead, thicko, cretin, idiot, moron, numbskull…. Ambrose knew them all. Harvey would claim his right to be king. He was the strongest, the fittest, the fastest. And he was convinced that every move he made, every decision he took, was the right one. By right he meant that it would lead to self-gain. That, to Harvey, was being intelligent. The rest of humanity he would convert into mere serfs, inferior beings with little or no initiative and even fewer brain cells. Harvey's defense would be predictable and simplistic: we deserve what we get.

But Ambrose realized he had no way of expressing all that. They were ideas that were clear enough in his own mind, but that would never find their way into coherent speech. He would muddle them up and choose the wrong vocabulary, he would be thrown off track by anything that Harvey said, especially if he didn't really understand the true meaning of it. And Harvey loved to confound him with long words and quasi legal jargon. So he would remain silent. Anyway, Spotty had warned him – don't listen to the slimy toad, he's too smooth talking for you, Bro, no offence, but the snake can also charm. Best not bother with any crap or he'll talk you out of it. Don't listen to him, Bro, close your ears, ignore him, he's a fucking lawyer after all, so it's all bullshit anyway. Elegant not eloquent. Got that?

The pause, the silence, gave Harvey a little hope. If Bro was going to shoot him he would have done so by now, surely? So he was bluffing. He wouldn't have the balls to just kill him in cold blood, yet he clearly wanted something. Well he would find out what it was that had driven him to this lunacy. The cinema clients would be turning up within the hour and he needed to get the cars ready in good time. He would have to sort out this incident with Ambrose as quickly as he could.

'Mr. Ork.'

He used his most authoritative voice. Very often the master's voice is sufficient in such cases. The man needed to know who was boss. There was an uneasy second or two while Ambrose shifted his position a little and re-aimed. Perhaps a slightly more reconciliatory tone was required.

'Ambrose. I, I ...'

What was he supposed to say? I didn't expect to see you? So

you got out of jail? So you have come to kill me? It was absurd. What was he to do, talk him out of it like a police negotiator? Like a fucking psychologist or something? Harvey was beginning to get annoyed. He puffed himself up. He would take the indignant stance. This man has forced his way into my home, stolen my gun, and now has the gall to threaten me in my own grounds. Outrageous. He would deal with this dimwit once and for all, get him put away in a mental institution, lock the door and throw away the key. What a complete idiot.

'Now listen to me. That is a very valuable gun.'

The only sound was the vaguely distant twittering and trilling of suburban wildlife. Both men held their ground.

'Do you realise that breaking and entering is a very serious crime?'

Bro's silence was unnerving, but he charged on.

'How did you get in? And, and what on earth are you doing with that gun? If you shoot that thing it'll wake up the whole town. The police will be here in a shot.'

He hadn't meant the pun, and the fact that he had not realised that until he had spoken made him feel even less sure of himself. And Bro still standing there, feet well apart, the barrels aimed at his chest. He hadn't so much as flinched at anything Harvey had said.

'Look, if it's about...'

Then Ambrose interrupted him. It was time for his speech. It wasn't much, but it was his and he had to say it. He was shouting, he knew, but couldn't help it, and ended up rushing through his lines like an amateur actor at a rehearsal.

'You killed Sydney. You put the cable in the pool and made him go for a swim. You killed him and I got the blame.'

Harvey relaxed at the familiar sound of his ex employee's dumb tone. So that's what he wanted, to get it off his chest, to complain like a child about the harsh treatment life had dealt him. Poor little thing. It was pathetic. But how best to handle this? How to get the dickhead to lower that damned gun even for an instant? Should he accept the accusation, give Ambrose the satisfaction of being told, for once in his stupid life, that he was right? What did he want, to see him on his knees, or would a simple 'sorry' be enough? It was hot out there on the forecourt, and time was ticking on relentlessly. Harvey decided to take the bull by the horns.

'I am not in the habit of killing children. You had a fair trial. Who has put this nonsense into your head, for heaven's sake? And now, I suppose, you are going to kill me. Really Ambrose, do you think for one minute that you can get away with...?'

The shotgun blast hurled him back against the four wheel drive, splattering it with blood. Harvey died instantly, his chest destroyed by the shot. Spotty had warned Bro not to listen to that sweet talk. And who had said anything about getting away with it?

The body lay slumped against the car, his sunglasses still incredibly on top of his head. There was blood and bits of cloth everywhere. Bud and his gang would not be wanting the vehicle now.

Harvey had been right again, the sound of that shotgun blast was enough to raise the dead. Bro had been warned about how to shoot such a gun. First Brendan had shown him how to hold one, how to stand, how to take aim. Then Spotty had explained about the kick back and the breathing techniques involved. But he had not expected such a deafening noise. The police would probably not take more than a few minutes to arrive, so he had to move fast.

He would now put into action his own part of the plan. It was something he had not discussed with anyone, something he could confess to no-one. It was the result of hours of contemplation, of soul-searching, all on his own without the aid of Spotty or Pet or anybody else. He had thought about it until he was one hundred percent sure. Now he was convinced - it was a better plan.

Looking down on Harvey's crumpled corpse he felt no remorse. He had wondered about that, how he would react to taking someone's life, if it would be as clinical and detached as it sounded when he went over the plan in his head or with Spotty in his cell. Often things are not like they sound on paper, and maybe, once it was too late and Harvey lay dead on the ground, he would suddenly repent, break into tears or cries of anguish, fall to his knees and beg forgiveness. It was possible; he had seen it happen in films. But no. He imagined how Harvey would have felt if things had worked out the other way round, if it had been Ambrose doubled up against the car in a pool of blood. He would have said 'you lose, moron', or something along those lines. Then he would have called the police so that the mess could be cleaned up as quickly as possible. It would have been a triumph, one idiot less. Well Ambrose felt the same.

He clicked open the gun and reloaded. It was a better plan. Better for Spotty, as this way nobody would bother to look any further, no over-energetic detective would try to trace Bro's movements over the last few days. No raid on the Bandstand bar, no cordoning off Myra's house. Nobody incriminated. There would be no need. It would be tidy and conclusive. For Pet, too. How could he leave her in such a pickle? Imagine it, her brother on the run, a murderer in the family. She would want to help, to hide him, to feed him. She would want to commit perjury to save his skin, would do anything to keep her younger brother out of danger and preferably out of jail. No, he couldn't ask that of her, it was too much. She had a new life now in Wollbury, with that Doug. He would pray for her.

He had thought of Andrea as well. The poor woman had no idea that her second husband had been killed, was slumped at his feet right now. Hadn't she suffered enough? What a life! Swathed in luxury yet hounded by tragedy. First happy-go-lucky Sydney driving straight into that tree, then... her son. Her only son. So young, so sweet. He didn't know if she really thought that he had been to blame for that or not. He hoped not, he liked to believe not. She certainly had never said anything bitter to him as far as he could recall. Now Ambrose had taken away the only thing she had left. One loud blast and she was alone. He could not add to that pain. She did not deserve to go through the rest of her life wondering who had killed Harvey, if it had truly been Ambrose or if it had been some other intruder, or if the killer was still on the loose, prowling the grounds at night, stalking her. She would have nightmares and continually think that she was next. It would make it impossible for her to start again and that would be unfair, because Ambrose had never wanted to harm Andrea. She'd been hurt enough as it was.

So to the final phase. He checked his weapon once more. It snapped open and closed firmly as before. He would now take his own life. He would aim the barrels at his face, propping the gun under his chin so that the blast would rip his head off. He needed somewhere to lodge the butt. The car would be the best idea. With one foot he nudged the base of the shotgun towards the tyre of the rear wheel. Once it was snugly in place he would be able to go through with the last part of his plan. He had to make sure it was well jammed, or the retort, yes, that was the word Spotty had used, retort. Or the retort could mean that he would miss his target. That could not happen. He must not survive, especially not terribly disfigured. What a horror. A mutilated murderer that needs constant medical attention. A double monster. The butt tended to slide a little on the gravel, he was not happy. .

He pulled open the back door and tried to find a slot somewhere between the seat and the floor, but the surfaces were too smooth, too curved in design, and the gun slid about dangerously. He needed something that would not move. Like Harvey.

He jammed the gun into Harvey's waist. Luckily Harvey's face was turned away and covered in blood, or perhaps Ambrose would have had a few qualms about using his body for support. It worked. Now all he had to do was pull the trigger and this drama would be over. He felt a sigh of relief at that. He was tired now, exhausted after all his anxiety. He had hardly slept the night before, continuously worrying over every detail. The incognito bus journey out to Langley, breaking into Haute House, going for the gun. Not to mention all those memories. He had feared that something would go horribly wrong, it usually did. Maybe he'd catch the wrong bus, or get off at the wrong stop and lose his way. Or he'd bungle the burglar alarm. Or Harvey would have new dogs that would chase him away. Who knows, maybe the guns would not be there anymore, or maybe there'd be no ammunition. Harvey could call it all off, or enter the house and smell a rat. Christ, he might even have suddenly lurched at Bro and wrestled the weapon from his grip. It could have been Ambrose Ork lying there up against that wheel. But no, it had all gone according to plan. He had comfortably and competently accomplished what he had set out to do. Now all that remained was to put into action his own part of the plan, his individual addition, his personal creation. And ironically Harvey was going to help him.

He was satisfied. The twin barrels sank into his neck just above his Adam's apple, the other end was firmly wedged below Harvey's expensive belt. He tried to shift it, shaking it with both hands on the long barrels. It was firm enough. He reached for the trigger. The gun cut into his neck as he tried to stretch his hands and his fingers to their utmost, straining to feel the trigger unit. He pulled away and checked the situation. Maybe he needed to try just a bit harder. Or perhaps he needed to shift his position, try with the other hand. Once more he jammed the gun under his chin and stretched out for the trigger mechanism. It was no good. Try as he might he could not reach. With dismay he realised that his arms were too short. Harvey's fucking special. There had to be another way.

He was beginning to panic now. The police would surely be there at any minute, and he could not let himself be caught alive. He fell to the ground. Maybe if he took his boots off he would be able to use his toes to fire the damn thing. He ripped them off, grabbed the shotgun, and started rolling over in the gravel, trying to find a plausible position. This time he stuffed the butt under Harvey's legs. Lying on his side he manoeuvred until he felt his toe on the trigger. But now the barrels pointed more at his nose than under his chin. His chest seemed to push the barrels up and away from him. If he wasn't careful he'd blow away the best part of his face but nothing else.

He sat up again and examined the scene. There was nothing he could do. Either he sawed off the shotgun or he made his arms grow. How could he have been so foolish? It was simply something he had not taken into account. He thought now that if he had gone over this with Spotty first... But it had to be a secret or Spotty would not have wanted to be a part of it. So there he was, sitting on the forecourt next to Harvey's dead body, clutching a ridiculously long-barrelled shotgun which he could not figure out how to turn on himself. He could shoot himself in the foot, but there was no way he could take his own life.

Unsure what to do next, he leant back against the four wheel drive next to Harvey and waited patiently for the police to arrive. They'd know what to do. What a mess. For once he had decided to think for himself and make his own decisions, and look where it had led him.

He should have known better.